SNOWED IN FOR CHRISTMAS

A FUN, FEEL-GOOD HOLIDAY ROMANCE

KIMBERLY KREY

Candle
House
Publishing

Snowed In For Christmas; A Fun, Feel-Good Holiday Romance Novel

This is a work of fiction. Names, characters, businesses, places, events, locales, and incidents are either the products of the author's imagination or used in a fictitious manner. Any resemblance to actual persons, living or dead, or actual events is purely coincidental.

❀ Created with Vellum

CHAPTER 1

Easton cinched up his laces with double knots on each winterized mountain boot.

"A bet's a bet, Easton," his sister said through the phone line, "so you better man up or I'll..."

Easton clenched his jaw tight. He could picture her now, standing beside her kitchen sink with a fist poised on one hip, scrambling for a word strong enough to scare him into following through.

"I won't name the baby after you," she finally threatened.

Easton snatched the phone off the bed, keeping it on speaker mode as he headed toward his closet. "I never asked you to name him after me, Chantelle," he said. "You wanted to do that all on your own."

"Well, I *won't* want to if you don't follow through. Can't name him after someone who doesn't keep his word."

Great, the guilt card. He only wished he couldn't feel the hot sting of it in his gut. It would make him a liar if he backed out now. Unless he could get his sister to see how ludicrous the idea was in the first place. It was easy enough for *him* to see—five bachelorettes at a resort with twenty-five bachelors. Talk about a recipe for heartache and disaster. Not to mention humiliation—it would be broadcast for all of America to see, for crying out loud.

"Why can't you just…*get* that this whole dating show thing is the *opposite* of anything I would ever want to do?"

"Why?" she snapped. "Because you're scared of being on TV?"

"I'm not *scared* to be on TV, I'm strongly opposed to it, but that's not even the biggest factor. I don't trust crappy manufactured dating setups. I don't, I'm sorry."

"So," Chantelle said. "You should have thought of that before you made that deal with me. I worked my butt off to raise more money than you did and I'm thirty weeks *pregnant*. Do you have any idea how much harder it was for me than it was for you?"

Wow, she was really playing this one up, wasn't she? His mind flashed back to the months he'd spent raising money for their wilderness survival camp—a camp he and his sister founded and operated together. The facility was designed to help struggling teens and young adults, providing top-of-the-line care and counseling while teaching outdoor survival techniques. Something that took a lot of money to run. The annual fundraiser allowed them to reduce the price for certain candidates and even offer the occasional free help for those who qualified. And God bless the few kids who *did* qualify, they needed the help all the more.

Still, after all that he'd done—and he'd done a lot—Easton

was shocked to find his sister had outdone him by a whopping sixty thousand dollars.

"I'm sure it was…very difficult," he allowed. "But come on, how about I just agree to…I don't know, activate the profile you made for me on that horrible dating network."

"It's *not* horrible, and I can't believe you're even talking about skipping out on this. The network is sending someone to the center for your final interview in just a few days. Which means whoever's interviewing you already has plane tickets and probably a million other things planned around it. So suck it up, be a good sport, and do the freaking interview. Heck, maybe they won't even pick you and you've thrown this big tantrum for nothing."

Easton rolled his eyes as he flung open his closet door. He grabbed a stack of fresh tees and a few wool sweaters before tossing them toward his duffle bag on the bed. He kept one of the sweaters and shrugged into it, switching the phone from his right hand to his left as he pushed his arms through the sleeves.

He straightened up as an idea came to mind. The interview could be his ticket out. At this point, he was only a finalist. If he botched the interview, he'd be eliminated and Chantelle couldn't be mad at him.

"You're right," he said, hurrying over to his dresser and resting the phone there. He grabbed an extra pair of jeans, a few pair of boxer briefs, and a pair of thermals too. "I can't back out this late. It'd be rude." He snatched up some wool socks next and spun to pack them into his bag.

"Exactly," Chantelle said. "Standing up the network, forcing people to scramble, that's unacceptable. We're better than that."

She was right, but for a reason he couldn't explain, the

comment struck a nerve. Perhaps it was because Easton *had* considered leaving Channel 13 high and dry. He didn't like the slight jab at his character, as merited as it might be.

His other line gave out a buzz. A quick peek at the screen showed just who was calling. "Speak of the devils," he mumbled. "I've got a call coming in. Just a minute." He tapped the screen to take the call. "Hello?"

"This is Ivy Ingles from Channel 13 calling to confirm our twelve o'clock appointment for Monday afternoon at the Front Range Survival Center." She sounded young. And while her voice was pleasant, the polished approach made him bristle.

"I'll be there," he assured. "How many will be in your crew?"

"Oh, no fancy production crew this round," she said. "Just me. The interview is to help the production team determine who will go on to the show. It won't be aired or anything."

Easton felt himself relax at the news. "No kidding?"

"No kidding. So you'll be there?"

"Yeah. In fact," he added, spinning to sit on the bed. "I'm heading out there right now."

"Wait—this soon? The place is covered in snow, isn't it?"

He grinned. "So?"

"So, it's an outdoor campsite from what I understand."

"We've got yurts."

"Yurts?"

"Picture a tall, circular hut with a cone roof," he explained.

Some paper rattling ensued. "Oh, yes. *You're* the one we're interviewing in front of one of the outdoor structures, it says. I guess that's what they mean. Perfect."

"I'm *the one?*" he echoed. "How many interviews are you doing? Don't tell me you're covering all fifty of the finalists."

She chuckled, but it sounded more like a choke. "Heavens no. Most of the interviews were done earlier in the month. I've got just five this time. I'm headed to Arizona to get my second interview."

"From LA?" he asked, not sure why he was curious.

"From Vegas, actually. A pro gambler," she said.

"You don't say? People do that for a living?"

"Apparently."

He smiled, then remembered that he was supposed to blow the interview, not make friends with the chick interviewing him before they even had the chance to meet.

"You know," he said, lowering his tone, "we're supposed to see a real blizzard in the next few days. You might have to camp out in one of the yurts with me over the holiday. But don't worry, if that happens, I'm sure I can keep you warm somehow."

If Chantelle was listening to the call, she'd *know* he was trying to blow it. Easton never spoke to women in such a way.

The woman on the other end of the line cleared her throat. "Save it for the contestants, sparky," she quipped. "I already have a plane ticket to fly home after our interview and I intend to make it there in time for Christmas Eve no matter the weather."

Huh. Why did he like her response so much? He guessed it was because it's just how he'd want his sister to reply if some creep was coming onto her. And he had to hand it to this Ivy chick, the play on words with the name she'd called him—his last name was Sparks, after all—showed a good amount of wit. Still, Easton had a first impression to ruin.

"Sounds like you have an *in* with Mother Earth, Ms. Ingles.

If that's the case, maybe it'll be all sunshine and rainbows for you. You'll fly out on a sunbeam, and once your plane is safely on its way, the storm will descend once more."

The cricket worthy silence said his comment struck home.

"I'll see you at twelve o'clock on Monday, Mr. Sparks. Goodbye."

An odd blend of satisfaction and guilt settled over him as the line shifted back to the call with his sister.

"Was that them?" Chantelle blurted. "Was that the station?"

"Yes," he said. "It was Ivy Ingles. She's the one who's going to interview me. She just finished up with some pro gambler in Vegas and now she's headed to Arizona to interview heaven knows who."

"Pro gambling is a thing? Huh."

His mind drifted back to the way this Ivy put him in his place, telling him to save it for the bachelorettes. Little did she know he had no intention of getting that far.

"So she's still planning to meet you out at the property?" his sister asked.

Easton tossed some deodorant, his toothbrush, and some toothpaste into the duffel bag next. "Yep."

"Good. I can't believe how well the timing worked out too. We don't have a group in session, but you'll be up there anyway, getting ready for the winter crew."

"Yeah, funny how that worked," he said, heavy on the sarcasm. Shortly after the New Year, they'd welcome a new group of struggling young adults into their winter survival program. Hence, Easton's four day getaway to secure and prepare the yurts.

"All right then," he said, zipping up the duffel bag and hiking it onto his shoulder. "I'm heading there now. It's supposed to storm, so I figure we can just…go inside the main office and do the interview in the commons area of the lodge. Or maybe at my desk."

"What?" Chantelle screeched. "*No.* You can't do it inside. The setting is supposed to represent you in some way. You're an outdoor survival specialist, not some dork at a desk."

"I work at a desk," Tim, Chantelle's husband, hollered in the background.

"You know what I mean," Chantelle hissed. "If you're going to attract the right woman, you need to present the real you."

He wasn't planning to attract any woman. "You know they don't have a big camera crew," Easton said. "It's just one woman doing the interview and the recording both. Probably from her phone."

"If you can't do it outside the yurt, do the interview from inside the structure, okay?"

Easton nodded. "Yeah. I guess that would work."

"It will *totally* work." She squealed then. "Ah! I'm so excited to see how it goes."

He channeled his best monotone voice. "Yippee. Me too."

"You just wait," Chantelle said, her voice full of fluctuation and joy. "One day, you're really going to thank me for this."

"Doubt it."

"No, you will. Wow, I can't believe you're actually going to be on that show."

Easton was halfway through the kitchen when her words stopped him cold. His boots gave out a squeak against the tile floor as he froze in place.

"You said this was an interview to *see* if I move on to the end. There are still fifty guys, right?" The blood had definitely drained from his head. His hands went numb. It felt like the moment he'd come face to face with the black bear beside the creek last year. The one time he'd left his bear horn in the tent.

"Yes, of course," Chantelle said. "But there's no way they're going to let a bachelor like you slip between their fingers."

Easton regained feeling in his hands. He sighed, relief tricking clear down to his toes. "Well, believe it or not, sister dear, they might not find me as charming as you do."

"You just don't know what a catch you are." She followed the comment with a loud yawn.

"Yes, I've got you riveted even in conversation," he mumbled.

"Sorry," she said. "It's the baby, not you. I swear I get more tired by the day. Just ten more weeks to go, right?" Another yawn sounded.

Easton grinned, noting the same conflicting emotions that surfaced each time he thought about being an uncle. Some aspects he liked and looked forward to; others, not so much. It felt like a big responsibility, especially since the little guy would be named after him.

"Well, you go take your nap," Easton said. "I'm headed out to the grounds to see what condition the yurts are in. I'll make a list of anything we need and, as you suggest, hold the interview in one as well."

"Perfect. How long are you staying again? You'll be here for Christmas, right?"

"Right," he said with a nod. "Of course. I'll head out on Christmas Eve."

"What about the storm? If it's as bad as they think, you

better leave right after your interview. You don't want to be stuck there over Christmas Day."

The truth was, the idea didn't sound so bad. Chantelle and Tim were gracious hosts, but did they really need a third wheel butting into all of their holidays? Especially now that they had a baby on the way.

"Easton?"

"Sure," he said. "But I doubt we'll see the kind of blizzard they're warning about." Though the very image of such a blizzard gave him a rush. How awesome would it be to weather that kind of storm from a fire-warmed hut like the yurt?

"Well, if it is, you better head out with the gal from the station. She'll be anxious to get back to her family too. Can't believe they're interviewing people the day before Christmas Eve. They're cutting it close."

"Networks like that don't care about Christmas. Unless it puts money in their pockets, that is."

"Always the skeptic," she accused. "Well, at any rate, thank you, for holding up your end of the deal. I can think good things about you again."

His face scrunched up. "Jeez, you're making me picture you hovered over a voodoo doll with comments like that."

"Oh, hush." They might not be on a video chat, but mentally, Easton could see Chantelle's eye roll.

He hovered his thumb over the device, ready to say goodbye and disconnect the call, when his sister spoke up once more.

"You know something?"

"Yeah?" he said, shifting his weight from one foot to the next.

"This really might be it, you know? You doing this interview, this show…it might be how you find your match."

How he finds his match. Easton tried to make the comment settle into his mind. Tried to make it fit into the box of things he believed in, but there was no way. He'd have better luck forcing a square peg into a triangular slot. But that wasn't what Chantelle wanted to hear, and he didn't want to provoke an argument. "Maybe," he forced himself to say. "See you in a few days." He disconnected the line before he could hear any hint of satisfaction from his optimistic-sounding reply.

Irritation pushed through him like a life force. Adding angst to every movement as he tossed soup cans, dried jerky, nuts, and drink mixes into his pack. An airtight container sat on his counter—the cinnamon rolls his neighbor left him. Beside that stood the jar of moonshine peaches another neighbor, Jerry, handed out each year. Easton wasn't sure what the guy used to make his *moonshine,* but those peaches sure packed a punch.

May as well take them along too. There would be plenty of water on the grounds, so he grabbed a refillable canteen and flung open the door to his garage.

The sight of his rugged looking Jeep earned a reluctant grin. Dang, he loved that thing. It was the one luxury he'd allowed himself, allowed since it helped him get around on the grounds no matter the weather or terrain.

Perhaps the next few days wouldn't be ruined after all. Sure, his sister had won this one, and now, for integrity's sake, he'd have to at least do the stupid interview. But Easton wouldn't let that spoil his weekend on the snow-covered ground with nothing but the fox and cougar to greet him.

Once he settled on the best approach, he'd focus on the

wonders ahead of him. The peace and tranquility he'd enjoy as he spent the night in one yurt after the next throughout the campground.

But for now, he decided, as he settled behind the wheel, he'd tackle the pesky little chore that sat in his way: What was the best way to botch an interview for becoming one of America's next TV bachelors?

CHAPTER 2

Four interviews down and one to go.

Ivy let that encouraging truth seep into her mind as the plane touched down. Just out the window, beyond the tarmac, a thick layer of white, puffy snow covered the ground from every visible angle.

The overhead announcement gave passengers a quick weather report that matched the image, along with the go-ahead to take her phone off airplane mode, something she wasted no time doing. The small device pulsed and buzzed with a slew of incoming texts. She assessed the damage—thirty-eight text messages. Only the Ingles family text group could tally up that many texts within a forty-minute flight.

Yet before she could scroll through them, her phone started to ring.

Nancy, the screen read. Great. Nancy was the other gal gunning for the position she hoped to score. The woman matched Ivy's eagerness to get the job, and was close to her skillset too, but one thing they didn't have in common was Nancy's out-of-bounds behavior when it came to getting what she wanted. Which meant Ivy had to really watch her back.

"Hi there, Nancy," Ivy said, bringing the phone to her ear.

"I'm all done," the woman gloated.

Of course she was. Ivy could picture her wrapping her signature wad of green gum around her finger as she spoke. "And get this..." she said, her loud gum-chewing enhancing the mental image. "I even snuck in an extra."

Ivy's eyes went wide. "An *extra?* You can't do that."

"Marsha gave me the clear. I snapped a pic of him at the airport after telling him a little about the competition, and Marsha liked the look of him so she said if I could get him to fill out the paperwork and sign the contract, we could put him in the final fifty. Well, fifty-one now."

"That's..." Annoying, she wanted to say. "Awesome."

"I know it is. And you should see my interviews. I have got some *live* ones, I'm telling you. These guys are pouring their hearts out. I've always been told I'm easy to talk to. I feel like this kind of confirms it."

"Yeah, Nancy, you're something special." She hated the sarcasm in her own voice. Ivy had to hand it to her—Nancy was good at what she did. "I better get going," she added. "We're getting ready to step off the plane."

"You back home for the holidays now?" Nancy asked.

She wished. "Not yet. I just landed in Denver, but I fly back out this evening after my final interview. A really handsome guy named Easton—"

"You're crapping me, right?"

Another overhead announcement picked up—some caution

about an incoming blizzard. "Crapping you about *what?*" she asked, covering her other ear to block out the noise.

"You're actually in Denver right now? You're never going to get out of there today. Or tomorrow. Heck, you're probably going to be stuck there for the whole week. Bye, bye Christmas with the family. Hello to a holiday at the airport with stranded strangers and—"

"I've really got to go, Nancy. Talk to you soon." Ivy quickly disconnected the line. That woman was an instigator if she'd ever known one. Ivy had never met someone so desperate to toot their own horn. It was pathetic. On and on and on she went about how wonderful she was. As if no one in her life had ever done it for her.

A small but stinging ache snuck into Ivy's heart at the thought. That was probably true. And didn't Ivy, as wonderful as her family might be, relate to that very thing? She was the youngest, after all; every accomplishment she'd made was old hat. There were always bigger and better things happening.

If she were being honest, it's what made this promotion so important. Ivy had been dying to share some spectacular news with her three siblings—the pediatrician, the lawyer, and the dental hygienist.

Which reminded her of all the texts she'd missed.

Ivy hurried through them, hoping to get the gist without having to read each and every text. Danny, her oldest brother, had set things into motion with a picture of the twins in matching Christmas PJs. Ronny sent a family pic, complete with his wife Joelle, their baby, and an ultrasound to represent the one on the way. Her only sister, Jackie, sent pics of her and her new husband, Paul, a staged kiss beneath the mistletoe.

Happiness and Christmas joy oozed off each photo. Each family was, in a word, *perfect*.

This was yet another demonstration of how...*behind* Ivy was in the game of life.

Her shoulders slumped. Her chest ached. *Oh, no.* This is how her slumps began. If she let it, this very moment could disrupt that neatly stashed fear of hers. A fear based on years of dating experience—a practice she'd hit pause on over the last year and a half. It was just that, in her experience, men were only interested in the beginning.

Once she let them in, once she really opened her heart to them, they lost interest. The most recent and traumatizing example was her relationship with Matt Shields from Channel Two—he'd thoroughly broken her heart. He'd told her, of course, that he didn't want to be tied down, but then he'd gone on to marry just six months later.

The fear was then, that if she ever let anyone see that deeper side of her, they'd lose interest.

Which is why you're not even dating right now, Ivy, so get over it.

That was true. She'd hold tight to her no-dating-until-she-got-her-promotion policy, which took any shred of pressure or false hope off her back. So...back to the texts.

A deep sigh slipped through her lips as she scrolled past dozens of oohs and ahhs over the pictures until she spotted her name in the mix.

Danny: Where's Ivy?

Ronny: Probably working.

Jackie: She is. But she said she'll be here in time for the Christmas Eve party.

Dad: She better be.

Mom: She will be. She's just trying to get that promotion. Let's all send prayers and good thoughts her way while she travels.

Danny: Is that real mistletoe, Jackie? Taya says she wants some.

The conversation went back to the mutual adoration of everyone and their families. Even Mom and Dad got in on the action and sent a picture of the two cuddled up with hot cocoa, the old Christmas tree with its handmade ornaments in the distance.

Ivy ignored the small prick of loneliness she felt while scrolling past the images. She had a career to focus on before she even thought about love, she reminded herself. To satisfy her family members, and to show that she was, in fact, doing important things of her own, she snapped a picture of herself on the plane with the small window at her back.

Ivy: Entering a winter wonderland to interview potential bachelor number five for America's Looking for Love show. I love the pictures of you all. See you on Christmas Eve.

She hit send, sighed out a deep breath, and muted the text conversation to prevent her phone from buzzing while she hurried about the airport to catch her cab. At once, she thought back on her conversation with Easton Sparks, her next and final subject.

I'm sure I'll find some way to keep you warm. Too bad he'd had to spoil his otherwise good first impression. The guy's picture and bio had seemed so promising too. Turned out he wasn't so different from the others. She recalled the way Leonard, the pro football player from Phoenix, rested his hand on her knee as he came up beside her on the bleachers. *"How about we go back to my place and I'll show you my trophies..."*

Had she come off as a woman who'd actually say yes to that proposal? It was insulting. Sure, he had a lot of great qualities, but his let's-hit-the-sack come-on was anything but flattering. Then there was the cowboy; he hadn't missed his chance to ask her out either, though he'd been more respectful. Even the gambler had rolled the dice, asking her to stick around and be his good luck charm through his upcoming rounds of blackjack.

Of course, she couldn't flatter herself over encounters like that. First of all, these men didn't even know Ivy. And second, they wanted to get on the show, which meant they were looking for an "in." Not that she could blame them. Of the four candidates, only the teacher from Wyoming hadn't come onto her. Though the man had spoken so quietly she might have missed it if he had.

A dose of pity rushed through her at the recollection. The poor guy might know how to address a classroom of middle school kids, but speaking directly to a woman with a camera had proven to be a different story. She doubted he'd go into the show's final round, but she'd been wrong before. Sometimes the network was less interested in perfect matches than they were in entertaining television. Sadly, one didn't always equal the other.

Hopefully he'd end up with the right woman eventually.

Similar thoughts filtered through Ivy's mind as she retrieved her luggage, weaved her way out of the airport, and stepped onto the bustling sidewalk. She shivered, immediately assaulted by the frigid air. Hadn't her time in Montana and Wyoming prepared her enough? Talk about terrible. Another mean shiver rocked her body as she propped her carry-on bag onto her standing suitcase and hurried to unzip it before her fingers froze.

Ivy had been foolish to think the name brand coat she'd bought in the sunny city of LA would protect her against the elements. Made of faux leather, the tan coat might be better called a jacket were it not for the fuzzy layer of white lining the inside. A lining that made it feel soft and warm in the toasty LA climate. Sadly, it was not made for weather like this.

Luckily, she hadn't spent a whole lot of time outdoors during her trip thus far. After each interview, she'd been quickly ushered back to her hotel in an amply heated cab. True, she wouldn't be staying in a hotel tonight; instead, Ivy would head straight back to LA where frostbite and flurries did not exist. She could hardly wait.

Once she'd shrugged into the thing, she secured her bags and waved down a cab. "Where are you going?" the man behind the wheel said as she hurried toward the trunk he'd popped open.

She worked to hoist her luggage into the trunk, then closed it with a *humph,* noting a special ding from her phone. Only one number made her phone give her that unique alert, and that was Marsha Langston's.

Ivy hurried to read the text as she climbed into the back seat.

Marsha: Thanks for sending your last four interviews. They're great, but the one I'm looking forward to most is Easton Sparks'. His resume and photos are something else...he'll have America going crazy! Make that interview count! I know you will. A kiss face closed out the text.

A rush of adrenaline surged through her at the woman's

confidence. This was her shot. Her chance to show Marsha that she deserved this promotion more than anyone. Her shot to prove that…that taking a year and a half dating hiatus had actually been driven by determination and not fear. But to prove that to whom—herself?

Ivy set her attention to her phone and quickly texted out a reply. She kept it short and sweet, the way Marsha preferred: *I won't let you down.*

And she meant it. Ivy would make this interview, the one with the very handsome-sounding flirt from Front Range, her best yet.

"Miss?" came the man up front. "Your destination?"

She hit send and lifted her chin to address the cab driver.

"You should really have a screen-locking feature on your phone," he said with a nod. "My kids got onto my social media once. Posted some *very* inappropriate things."

Ivy tipped her head in question, then glanced down at her phone. "I deactivated that feature on purpose. I don't have any kids."

"Oh. Where you headed?"

"Sorry. Front Range, please."

"*Front Range*?" His black, bushy eyebrows shot up, echoing the panic she'd heard in his voice. "Why?"

"I'm doing an interview. There's a survival camp there," she added.

Only the man didn't start driving. Instead, he propped an elbow on the back of the seat and spun to look at her. "You know there's a blizzard coming…" he said.

"So I've heard. But you guys are used to blizzards, aren't you?" Heck, it was Denver, for crying out loud.

"We're used to *snow*," he corrected. "Blizzards...I don't think I could make it very far in the canyon with conditions like that. Especially as the road starts to narrow..." He shivered. "Is there any way you could have someone meet us part way? Someone with chains on their tires, perhaps? We're looking at buckets of snow. Clear-up-to-your-*roof*-in-a-matter-of-days snow."

What, was this guy from Hawaii or something? She ducked to take a look at the freeway overpasses. "It looks like the roads are clear to me."

"Sure, right here they are. The plows are going over it nonstop. But where you're going, they won't be. In fact, when the blizzard *really* hits, you won't be able to see your own hand in front of your face. They'll probably send us all home within the next few hours is my guess."

A shock of fear shot through her. "Who? The cab company?"

He nodded.

"Send *all* the cab drivers home?"

He nodded once again. "It's a very bad storm, Miss. And with tomorrow being Christmas Eve and all, they're encouraging people to get to the place they want to be on Christmas Day today, as they fear travel in the next few days might be difficult, if not impossible."

More fear rippled through her. If she was smart, she'd run right back into that airport and take the first flight out of there. But would that really be the wise thing to do after all?

No, because Ivy could *not* miss out on this interview. Likewise, she could also *not* get stuck in this heaven forsaken town where fingers froze into paralysis within seconds flat. *Claim it, Ivy. Claim what you want.* She took a moment to do just that. After all, reading the self-help book that focused on the importance of a can-do attitude is what had helped her become one of Marsha's top assistants. Now if she could just beat Nancy for that coveted spot.

"It's going to be fine," she told him, claiming that very outcome in her mind. *The storm will clear. I'll get the interview. I'll be home in time for Christmas Eve.* "Tell me how far you can take me. I'll have my…friend meet us there."

Of course, that meant she'd have to call Easton Sparks again. The man who'd suggested her positive thinking would produce sunshine and rainbows just for her. "On second thought," she said. "Pop the trunk. I'd rather take a rental vehicle. They have ones with four-wheel drive, I assume?"

"Yes, ma'am, they do."

"Fine then. Thank you for your help." At once, she was flinging open her door and hurrying to the back of the cab. It took her a moment to hoist the heavy suitcase from the confined space. She was rewarded with a smashed toe as it landed on her poor excuse for boots. The leather, ankle high boots did little to warm her feet and they, to her dismay, seemed to soak up moisture as quickly as she stepped into it.

She fought back a curse while yanking her case over the curb, barely pausing to lean down and tell the cab driver to have a merry Christmas. She hurried across the street then, pinching her thin coat together in the front to fight off the chill. The man at the rental place, after insisting she get every extra insurance coverage they offered, assured her she was doing the right thing.

"If anything can get you up to Front Range this time of year, this baby can," the round man assured while hoisting his pants from his lower hips to his upper belly.

"Thank you." Now there was just one last thing to do. Text Easton Sparks and let him know she was on her way. That way, if she got lost or stuck or stranded—and hopefully she would *not*—he could alert someone. Like the authorities to come and collect her dead, frozen body.

No, Ivy. Claim it. Things will be fine.

She tapped Easton's number into her texting app and typed out a quick message.

This is Ivy Ingles. The cab wouldn't take me all the way, so I'm driving there myself in a huge SUV. Please...

She paused there. Please, what?

Yet just as she began to consider her options, her thumb accidentally bumped the screen.

Oh no. Please don't...

The device let out a small but certain *swish*. A beat of paranoia rushed through her as she realized it sent before she was finished. She read over the sent message in a frenzy, assuring that auto correct hadn't done anything crazy. When she found that it hadn't, Ivy hovered her thumbs over the keypad once more, preparing to finish the last sentence of her text when a reply popped in beneath it.

A reply from Easton.

Please what, Ivy? C'mon, don't be shy...

She growled and shook her head. "I'm not replying to that at all," she declared. "He knows I'm coming. That's enough for now." And with that, she put her navigation app to work and headed toward her final interview.

She was just six miles into her forty-minute trek when another text came in. This one, also, from Easton. Had she not had her phone propped on the dash and, had his message not been so very short, Ivy couldn't have read the reply until she was stopped. As it was, the quick flash at the top of the screen showed her just what he'd said. Two short words that put a little warmth in her heart in the frigid day.

Drive safe.

CHAPTER 3

Why in heavens name did he have to have such a bleeding heart? The blizzard was coming in strong now, making it hard to distinguish one white-covered surface from the next. Some were higher, some were lower, some were close up and others farther away, but in the flurry of thick flakes, it was hard to decipher which was which.

"Where in the crud are you, Ivy?" he grumbled, hands clenched tight around the wheel. Two hours had passed. Two full hours. At best, it should have taken her no more than an hour, maybe an hour and a half to get from the main airport to the campground under conditions like these. He'd watched. He'd waited. But no one had come.

There'd been no point trying to call her. She'd have lost reception before hitting the mouth of the canyon. Only once she was close to the campground would she be able to get reception once more.

Without any visible tire tracks in either direction, the road was that much harder to see. Easton squinted his eyes, relying on memory once he recognized the very high structure to his right. Point High Rock. Okay, he wasn't that much further from the mouth of the canyon, which was both comforting and frightening. When would he spot this so-called *huge* SUV she was sporting?

But then it came into view. Kind of. The shape of such an SUV beneath a thin but thorough layer of snow. As he lowered his gaze, he spotted a set of glowing dots, muted by a coating of flakes as well. A sudden movement from the covered mound took him by surprise, until he recognized what it was—windshield wipers.

His own wipers, frantically sweeping back and forth, a hundred times to her one, gave him a glimpse of the woman behind the wheel before the snow took over once more.

A wave of relief pushed through him. She was okay, thank goodness. He had to hand it to her—the woman was ambitious. And, if his eyes hadn't deceived him through the blur of fogged glass and puffy flakes, she was fairly pretty as well.

Trouble was, as she'd likely discovered today if not many occasions prior, ambition like hers could land one in a whole heap of trouble.

Easton twisted the knob to the yurt and pushed his shoulder against it. Massive flakes covered every inch of him as he turned to motion the woman inside.

She hesitated, her eyes seeming to search the area for a blink.

"Go on in," he hollered over the whistling wind. He sighed out a breath of relief when she ducked her head and hurried inside. The ducking, she'd soon realize, wasn't necessary. The dwelling, a round, teepee type structure, had a ceiling roughly thirteen feet high. Each yurt held the basic necessities. Tools, kitchen supplies, seating, and a fireplace that safely funneled the smoke outside. As well as a port-a-potty just off each structure. It was as close to *roughing it* as they dared to get for their brave winter crew. Not that they didn't spend nights in snow caves too some of the time.

Ivy spun in place for a blink, eyeing her surroundings while shivering against the cold. "Does that port-a-potty I saw out there work?" she asked, still taking a slow turn.

"It sure does."

When she'd made it full circle, she pointed at him and let out a shock-laced laugh. "Your hair!"

Easton patted at the coated mass of snow atop his head. He raked a hand through the strands of his hair to break it up, and chunks of matted snow tumbled to the rug. He stole a quick glance in her direction. "You're lucky there's not a mirror in here," he said. "You'd have yourself a *real* laugh."

The smile fell off her face. Hesitantly then, she reached blindly to pat at her own head. Her eyes widened in shock, and then she laughed again. "Oh my gosh," she said, laughing some more. "I think I could make a snowball out of all this." She tipped her head to the side and began to shake it off. "Oh," she said suddenly, "should I be doing this outside?"

The look she turned on him took Easton by surprise. In truth, he was still stuck on the unexpected way she'd reacted to her messed up hair. In his experience, women from LA who dressed like her and talked like her…well, they didn't like getting their hair wet.

"What was that?" he had to say. In truth, after a wordless, white-knuckle drive home, and an also wordless venture from the Jeep to the hut, Easton wasn't sure what to expect.

"I probably shouldn't be letting all of this snow drop onto the floor in here," she said, trying to cup her hands to prevent the rest from falling.

Easton shook his head, surprised again that she'd even taken that into consideration. "No, it's all right. This floor covering is a blend of bamboo and polyester. It will dry quickly once I get a fire going."

"A fire?" She straightened up. "We don't have time for a fire. I've got to get your interview done so we can hurry back to the airport."

Now it was his turn to laugh. "Sorry, but that's not going to happen."

Ivy's jaw clenched shut. Her nostrils flared the slightest bit.

This was more what he expected.

"You don't understand," she said, tone more pleading than severe. "My promotion at the station depends on delivering these interviews on time. And second, it's my family's big Christmas Eve party tomorrow. I've never once missed that."

"Until this year," he assured her.

She studied him for a beat, allowing Easton to do the same with her. Most of the snow had fallen from her head, exposing the strands of her silky blonde hair, a nice compliment to her rather fair complexion.

Suddenly a soft, unexpected smile pulled at one side of her lips. "I'm probably coming across rude," she said. "I'm not trying to. So let's see if we can start over." She took a few deep breaths —the sort the staff therapists called calming breaths—and leveled a look at him. "My job is the most important thing to me right now. Most important, that is, next to my family…"

He nodded, then absently shot a glance at her left-hand ring finger. No ring.

"So when I booked these back-to-back flights to conquer all five interviews before Christmas, I did so because it will help me get the promotion. But I would never have done it, if I hadn't known I'd make it back in time to celebrate the holiday with my family, you know?"

Her voice had lost some of its steam. Her shoulders were starting to deflate. And her dark lashes glistened with moisture. The sight pulled at Easton's heart in ways he didn't want to think about.

"Yes, I…get that. That makes sense."

She let out a shaky breath. "Good. So all we need to do is get your interview done. I can shoot this one on my phone, the producer will totally understand, and then I need to get back to the SUV so I can hurry and get to the airport."

Was she insane? "I hate to be the one to break this to you, especially because it seems pretty *freaking* obvious, but there is no way you're making it back in time for your little party. So I suggest you make yourself comfortable, let me get a fire going, and—"

"I'm *not* staying the night with you," she blurted.

Easton winced. He deserved that remark after his little warning over the phone last week. "Fine," he said. "You can stay in your *own* yurt. Or you can sleep out in the snow with the wolves for all I care." He pointed toward the road they'd just come from. "What you *can't* do is get back in a vehicle and try to drive in that storm."

She had no idea how close to death they might have been had Easton not known that road with all of its narrow turns and steep cliffs. "Trust me when I say it's a very good thing you hadn't gotten any further than you did. You'd have hurled that SUV right off the cliff in the miles ahead."

Ivy turned away from him, still hugging herself against the chill. Her teeth were chattering, and her body shivered so much it made her breath hitch. Too bad he'd extinguished the fire in the last yurt to inspect the next. But this had been the plan all along. Spend a night in each to ensure they were all up to standard operation. No leaks, drafts, or dangers. A clear shield covered the yurt's rectangular skylight overhead, sending a uniquely white glow of light to the space.

It must be what made her skin glow as if she were some sort of angel. More like a devil in disguise, he mused. What else could he call a woman who seemed hell bent on putting his life at risk?

"It's just that..." she sputtered. "My family...it's not..." She shook her head and let the sentence drift off.

Was it just him or did she seem to be disoriented? His heart skipped out of beat. Perhaps she was nearing stages of hypothermia. "Please," he said, "take a seat and let me get a fire started. We can talk more once you get warmed up."

Ivy nodded, jutted a look over her shoulder, and then shuffled her way toward the bench against the wall. At last, she plopped onto the wooden surface.

A massive, and rather inexplicable, wave of relief pooled

over him as he watched her settle into place. *There.* Now he could make sure she was safe.

A sheepskin wrap hung on the hook at her side. A much larger bearskin rug hung beside it. Easton walked toward her, reached for the smaller of the two, figuring the bearskin would be too heavy for her to hold over her shoulders, and quickly wrapped it against his back.

Ivy glanced up at him, curious at first, but then her eyes narrowed into a sharp glare. "How chivalrous," she spat.

Easton rolled his eyes. "I'm warming it up for you," he assured her.

Her face softened then, and she shrugged with one shoulder. "Oh. You think you're so much hotter than me, do you?" She must have realized how that sounded because a laugh snuck up her throat.

Easton couldn't help but chuckle at the remark as well. "I'm definitely not hotter than you, Ivy," he assured. "But I am *warmer* than you." He wasn't sure how he'd meant the comment to come off. Was his objective to act like a jerk unnecessary now? She'd made it sound like the interview was due that night. And as much as he could send and receive texts, especially when he got closer to the office, there'd be no possible way for her to send large files from their current location.

Besides, he was used to caring for and protecting his little sister. He'd done it his whole life. No harm in treating his female company with some old fashioned hospitality. With that, Easton tipped his chin down, allowing the top edge of the sheepskin to come in contact with the bare skin along the back of his neck. Satisfied that he'd heated it up enough for her, he closed the gap between them with slow and cautious steps. He was basically a stranger to her, after all.

Her tiny shoes, a flimsy excuse for boots, disappeared beneath the bench as he neared.

He grinned. "Here," he mumbled, "this should be nice and warm for you." He quickly moved it from his back and onto hers, encouraging her to lift her hair off the back of her neck to get the full warmth against her skin. Instinctively, he rubbed his hands down the outside of it, over her shoulders and down her arms.

Hints of something warm and sweet, like vanilla, hit his senses. She smelled good. The realization was enough to make him step away from her.

"Wow, you really *are* hotter than me." She glanced up, pulling at either side of the sheepskin. "Thank you," she added, her gaze set on the small boots as they reappeared from beneath the bench.

"Sure," he said. "I'm going to get a fire started. But first, I need you to promise not to...make a run for it."

The woman looked up in surprise. "Where would I go?"

Easton shrugged. "I have no idea. You seemed pretty desperate to get back down the canyon, is all I mean."

"I *am*," she assured.

"Yeah well, just tell me you're going to stay put so I can go collect some wood. If you take off, I'll have to go on another rescue mission and I'd rather not do that."

The wind must have changed angles, because suddenly a loud whoosh and whistle echoed within the structure.

"Where do you have to go to get firewood?" she asked, her voice louder to carry over the noise.

"To a nearby storage shed," he said, making his way to the door.

"How nearby? It's not going to take very long is it?"

Oh, she was scared, he realized. Easton shook his head. "No."

She nodded. "It's just...you pointed out those animal tracks..."

Yes, he *had* done that with the moose tracks he spotted while they hurried from the Jeep to the yurt; perhaps that had been a bad idea. It was, to him, habit, since he was usually in training mode while on the campgrounds.

"You'll be safe in here," he assured her. "I'll be right back." He was halfway to the door when she spoke up again.

"Easton?"

He froze in place. "Yes?"

"Are you absolutely one hundred percent sure that there's no possible way I'll make my flight?"

Easton sucked in a breath and let it out before responding. He pictured the spoiled woman making his life utterly miserable in the hours ahead. Rounds of vicious blame, irritation, and sheer anger over missing her flight.

"Ivy," he said, keeping his back to her. "As much as I wish it wasn't true, the truth is that your flight, along with every other flight in the days ahead, has already been canceled." He hurried to the door, pulled it open, and uttered two final words before heading out into the cold. "I'm sorry."

CHAPTER 4

Ivy couldn't tear her gaze off the door of the yurt as she held tightly to the thick wrap Easton had warmed her with. Her mind was whirling with all that had taken place in the last few hours. Surely the magnitude of those moments would start to sink in. Like the long minutes that ticked by as she gripped onto the SUV's steering wheel, following a road that got lost in whirls of white. It had been much too dangerous to carry on, but she'd been too stubborn to turn back.

And it definitely *was* stubbornness that prevented her from turning around at that point. She'd even cursed the rock she'd run into, cursed it for stopping her in her tracks, until she realized that those tracks were no longer on the actual road. A road that soon would become narrow enough to throw her off the edge with one wrong move.

What Easton had said was true.

A sick, hollow sounding thud pulsed in her ears, throbbing against her temples as the magnitude started to sink in. Had Easton not come looking for her…she shuddered against the thought.

The tank could have easily run empty before the storm died. There'd been no data or WiFi service to speak of. Even as he escorted her from the rental to his Jeep, Ivy had left the suitcase behind, still foolishly thinking she'd come right back to her rental once the interview was done. Her clothes, makeup, laptop and chargers, all of it sat in the abandoned SUV, where *she* would still be if he hadn't come looking for her.

Easton was definitely brave to weather the elements as he'd done. Many would likely alert the authorities if they thought someone was lost in the storm, not go looking for them on their own. Especially if that someone was a complete stranger. Of course, Easton, with his job as it was, probably possessed a greater survival and rescue instinct than most.

Still, it could be that he was so anxious to get on the show that he couldn't fathom missing out on the interview. This was his shot and he wasn't going to miss out on it. It didn't exactly fit the picture she was getting from him, but Ivy nodded just the same.

Whatever his reasons were, she was very grateful to him. So why couldn't she have done a better job of showing it?

An image of Marsha Langston flashed into her mind. An achy burn followed, trailing from her head to her heart.

Crap! Crapitty crap crap! I will not let you down? She wished she could un-send that stupid text. "Ugh."

Why had she volunteered to do all five interviews when they

were spread out over five different states, more than *half* of which were covered in snow? Because she'd been trying to keep up with Nancy, that's why.

Her mind forced her back to her dilemma. *It was a matter of life and death, Ivy. What's a promotion compared to that?*

A chill crept up her back at the truth of those words.

Surely Marsha could appreciate her dilemma. Especially since Ivy had gone out on a limb when the cab driver refused to take her. And maybe there was a story here. It was said that Marsha, as cutthroat and cunning as she might be, was a romantic at heart. Hence, her fascination with matchmaking TV shows. If that was the case, she'd be eating up Ivy's troubled tale with a spoon. One of her very own bachelors, chivalrously swooping to the rescue of her *top* assistant.

Ivy rode on that high for a blink. Yes, Easton's heroic rescue would surely earn him a spot in the finals. But who was she kidding—his appearance alone would do that no matter *what* his personality was like.

Easton Sparks, with his masculine chiseled jaw, angular nose, and those well-defined lips, had a face made for the camera. Not to mention his physique...

Marsha was right to have her sights set on him. Soon every woman in America would too. The thought almost kindled a tinge of jealousy, but not quite. How could she be jealous about something she didn't want for herself?

Only as she considered the way he'd tossed the warm blanket over her shoulders—the feelings that had fluttered through her at his touch—that statement didn't exactly feel true. Even in recollection, a soft ripple of goosebumps trailed up her arms. She guessed it was because he was so…manly and attractive. Having his undivided attention on her…it made her heart race even in recollection.

He knows he has that effect on women—he has to.

A sudden thud sounded from the door. "Ivy," she heard.

An image of Easton holding a stack of wood came to mind. "Oh, yeah." Quickly then, she darted over to the door with one hand holding the blanket in place, and cranked the knob with her other hand.

A mass of sloshy snowflakes pelted her face, fueled by a loud and vicious roar of wind. Her brother had once aimed a leaf blower at her face while cleaning grass clippings off the driveway. The speed of this wind with its wet, frozen chunks made that encounter look like a gentle breeze on a summer's day.

Ivy clenched her eyes shut against the assault and stepped out of the way, her fingers still curled around the door's edge. Once Easton stepped into the dwelling with a hulking mass of wood, Ivy hurried to push the door closed behind him.

The wind—surprise, surprise—fought against her, but she wasn't about to give up without a fight. The storm had taken enough from her for one day. She wasn't about to let it take her dignity too.

With that, Ivy readied herself, positioning her shoulder in just the right place. At once, she forced her weight behind the action and shoved off, forcing the door to give way as she wished.

She sighed.

No more wind trying to knock her off balance.

No more snowflakes attacking her face.

"There," she said proudly, dusting off her hands for effect.

She met eyes with Easton, noting that he'd covered the wood stack with a tarp. Good thing, since it was drenched with snow. Sheesh, that stack must weigh a ton. She lifted her gaze in time to see his eyes come alive with…fear?

"Ivy!"

Suddenly the door pushed open with a blustering growl and rammed her upside the head. She wasn't sure which part she processed first, the pain, or the *source* of the pain. Whichever it was, it felt more like an axe than a door.

At once Easton, who stood before the fireplace, dropped the massive wood stack. Ivy felt the room spin as she moved a hand to her head.

"Are you okay?" He was right next to her now, Ivy knew that much, since she could feel his arms supporting her at either side. What she didn't know was why his voice sounded so far away.

"Ivy?" Even more faint this time.

The light was fading too, and soon, everything went black.

Ivy woke up to a waft of warmth along the left side of her body. A cracking fire added to the ambiance, soothing all of her senses at once. She sucked in a deep breath, appreciating the smoky scent, and wondered how her gas fireplace was producing such effects. But then a face flashed through her mind, along with a name—Easton Sparks.

At once, her eyes popped open. She shot up into a sitting

position and darted quick glances about the space. Yurt. She was in a yurt. There was the fire, there was the wood, but where was Easton? And why was her head throbbing?

Another quick scan had her coming up empty once more. A beat of panic tore through her. "Easton?"

"Right here," he said, voice low and even. She shot a look over her shoulder to see him seated beside a wooden table in a rocking chair. Without a shirt. *Holy muscles...*

"How's your head?" he asked, lowering his elbows onto his knees and scrutinizing her.

Ivy moved a quick hand to it—too quick. The thud against the covered wound felt like a knife stab. "Ouch..." *Oh yeah, the door...* She patted at the dressing. "Did you do this?"

He nodded, and a spot of warm appreciation seeped over her.

"Thanks."

"You've got to twist the knob on the door to make it stick," he said.

"Oh." It was all she could think to say.

He continued to scrutinize her for a bit, then huffed out a sigh. "You'll want to get out of those wet clothes."

Ivy's eyes widened. She patted at her coat and jeans. It seemed the left side had come close to drying, while the right side—the part further from the flames—was still drenched. "I don't have my suitcase," she realized.

"I have some thermals you can wear. They'll be much too big for you, but I've got a trick for that."

She furrowed her brows. "What kind of trick?"

"You know how the bottoms have those small snaps up the front?"

Ivy nodded.

"Instead of snapping them up, you tie them into a knot. It pulls the excess fabric and makes them fit more snug."

"Huh." Ivy did more nodding as she considered it. One glance at the impressive size of his figure had her wondering though. "What, did you have to borrow King Kong's once?"

"Something like that," he said with a laugh. But then he elaborated. "It's a trick I discovered while helping my baby sister keep warm at night. She didn't have any of her own and she was pretty little at the time."

"How much younger is she than you?"

"Two and a half years," he said.

She gave that some thought, her heart aching as she considered what his childhood might have been like. Was it simply lack of money that caused the strain, or had he and his sister been neglected? "Sounds like you were pretty young then too."

Easton shrugged and pulled a duffle bag off the table. "Let's get you some clothes. You can hang the wet ones next to mine along that rod, you see it?"

Ivy glanced up to see his sweater, a pair of khakis, and a very wrinkled tee shirt. As if he'd spent a long time trying to wring it out. "How'd your undershirt get the brunt of it?" she couldn't help but ask, tearing her eyes off the sight.

Easton was still hovered over his bag, setting items atop the table while searching some more. "I used it to sop up the blood."

A completely uninvited thrill rushed through her at his answer. Was he *kidding?* He'd actually ripped off his sweater, torn off his tee shirt, and used it to dab the blood off her head? And she'd *missed* it? Her chest and face filled with delighted heat. "That's so...*nice* of you."

He lifted his chin at last and tossed her a navy colored pair of thermal pants. The shirt came next. "I'm a survival specialist," he explained as she caught the clothing in turn. "It's all second nature to me."

Okay, could she just admit right then and there that Easton Sparks was seriously sexy? Everything about him was rugged and masculine and causing her to wish she was one of the lucky bachelorettes lined up for the show. She wasn't sure why it was suddenly so undeniably clear. Perhaps she was still woozy. Maybe she had a concussion. Or perhaps the injury had smacked the stubbornness right out of her head. Whatever the cause, Ivy was done pretending he didn't have an effect on her.

"I'll give you some privacy," he said, spinning his chair in the opposite direction so he faced the rounded wall.

He was chivalrous too. "Oh. Okay, I'll hurry." It was a good thing the thermals were thick and dark, not like the white, threadbare numbers she'd imagined. She was quick to stand in place and remove her coat, and then her shirt. Whether wet or dry, her bra and panties weren't going anywhere, so it was a very good thing both were dry. She was pleased to find that her phone had stayed tucked into place, safely within her bra and away from the elements.

The discovery made her recall the interview. Would he be willing to do it now before her battery died? She'd already shrugged into the large top. It felt nice and warm against her skin. She tore off her wet boots, drenched socks, and jeans next, paying no mind to the crumpled heap as she reached for the bottoms. Quickly, she stepped into one pant leg after the next, and yanked them up to her, well....

"Don't turn around," she said, "but these pants could probably go up and over my head."

"Roll them at the bottom a few times," he suggested, "then we'll see what we can do about the rest."

We'll see? Ivy shot a look over her shoulder to ensure he was still facing the wall. He was, of course, so she did as he said, rolling up one pant leg at the ankle, then the other. She decided to try a similar thing with the waist by gathering the loose fabric, folding it down once, and then cinching it into a knot. "It's huge," she said, staring at the softball-sized wad of fabric at her belly. "It's like I'm having a thermal baby," she laughed.

"You dressed?" Easton asked from his spot against the wall.

"Yeah, you can turn around." She fiddled with the hem of the oversized shirt, wondering if she could get it to cover the knot, but it only looked worse. *Who cares, Ivy?* An irritated inner voice came. But *she* cared. She was with one of the most seriously handsome men she'd met in person.

"Here," he said, moving toward her. "There's a way, if you don't mind me showing you, to make it more flat. My sister was a belly sleeper, so the big knot wouldn't do..."

He glanced down at the lump before setting his eyes on hers. They were brown. A gorgeous brown that reflected the gold of the flickering flames. "May I?" he rasped with a nod in her direction. "I promise to keep things...decent."

Ivy nodded, lifting her hands in surrender mode. Her heart thudded wildly out of beat as he approached the messy knot of fabric with his large hands. She glanced up at his chiseled chest, the muscled contours accented by the firelight's shadow, and felt her face flush with heat.

"Here," he mumbled, untying the mass. The back of his

warm fingers barely grazed her skin as he worked. As promised, he seemed to keep focused on not exposing anything below her belly button. "Folding the top down like that was good," he said, "but let's do that after we tighten it up. If we twist it once, cinch it real good, and then pull it back like this..." He gave each side a good pull. "Ah, looks like you're small enough I can actually just snap the top button in the back. Here, spin around."

She did as he said, another slight thrill darting through her as his hand cupped her hip. A rush of goosebumps rippled up her arms.

A tiny little click sounded. He proceeded to roll the waist down once, then twice. "There," he said. "All done. I used to give my sister a swat on her diapered butt when I was through, but I'll spare you."

She chuckled and glanced down, appreciating the way he'd managed to create a fairly flattened twist in the front. "Thank you."

Ivy combed her fingers through her damp hair, her mind already rushing back to the interview. She spun back to face him, but dropped her gaze to her bare feet. How would she be able to bring it up? As it was, he'd done enough kind things for her that the two were wildly off balance. Could she really pester him for an interview after all of that? And at a time like this?

Marsha's text shot to her mind. She didn't have much of a choice.

"I've got a pair of socks for you," Easton blurted, seeming to just notice her feet. He retrieved a thick pair of oatmeal-colored socks and hurried back over to her. "You could probably fit both of those tiny feet into one sock, but I wouldn't advise it."

She laughed.

"Might make dancing with me in the firelight a little..."

"Impossible?" she offered, trying to ignore the thrill that shot through her at the image of dancing with him.

"I was going to say awkward, but that works too."

"Well then," she said, plopping onto the bearskin rug he'd spread out beneath her, "I better give these little piggies their very own socks. Did you know that of the two-hundred and six bones in the human body, fifty-two of those bones are in the feet?"

"Seriously?" Easton piped.

"Yep. Twenty-six in each foot. Crazy, huh?"

Easton surprised her by taking a seat on the floor as well. "Yeah, that is."

Ivy shoved one warm sock onto her left foot, then moved to the right one, recalling another interesting tidbit. "Also," she said, "fingernails grow way faster than toenails—like three times faster—which is good because I can't imagine keeping up on pedicures if they didn't." She smoothed a hand over her sock-covered feet. They were warming already. "Ah, these feel wonderful." She glanced up to see him nod slightly, the look of satisfaction on his face. As if it were his job to keep her warm and dry and safe...

"Good," he said under his breath.

"Thank you," she added.

"Any time." His gaze drifted to her upper arm. "Looks like the neck of the shirt is a little big."

She glanced down to see that it had slipped off her shoulder. A blush rose to her cheeks as she slipped it back up to her neck —not that it had revealed anything. Inwardly, her mind was fixed on the developing mystery before her. It was just that, with Easton, she felt bad for bringing up the interview, but that didn't exactly make sense. If he were anything like the other bachelors, he'd be itching to get that next step out of the way. Which meant that by recording it before her phone died, she'd be doing *him* the favor.

So why didn't she get the impression that he *was* itching to do it like the others had been?

It was time to find out.

Ivy retrieved her phone and took a look at the screen to check the battery.

"We won't get service unless we head back to the lodge," Easton said, guessing at her intent.

"Oh, I'm actually wondering if we can do your interview. Before I run out of battery, that is."

His eyes widened. "Right now? With your phone?"

Ivy nodded. "It's just for the producers to make a final decision. It doesn't have to be professional. Ideally, I'd record it on two devices, but since the camcorder's in the SUV, we may as well just do this."

"Ah." He tipped his head back, then nodded a few times. "So we still have to do the interview, huh?" There was that sense of dread she detected.

"This is your chance to go to the final round," she couldn't help but say. "The others were thrilled about doing the interview, but I get the idea that you're not."

He didn't argue.

"Why is that?" she ventured.

Easton's handsome face pinched in contemplation. He

rubbed a hand over his stubble covered jaw, the look in his eyes reaching far off, distant places. Searching. Grasping.

Ivy felt herself lean closer with anticipation. What was going on in this guy's head? And why was it taking him so long to answer the question? Was he trying to think of what she wanted to hear? Was he afraid to speak the truth?

"Just be honest," she urged.

Easton cleared his throat and, at last, fixed his brown eyes right on her.

A splash of warmth hit her heart as it beat out of rhythm, as if trying to sync with his. She almost wished that it could. Perhaps the connection would give her glimpse at the inner workings of his mind. The mind of that strong, quiet, heroic type.

"The honest truth is," he started, bending his leg to prop an arm on his knee, "I lost a bet. Doing a show like this reality bachelor whatever…I can't imagine anything worse."

What!

Ivy couldn't tell which part of his confession shocked her more. His outright candor or the fact that this perfectly manly specimen did not want millions of women swooning over him for years to come. Sure, she'd sensed his aversion, but she'd assumed he'd prove her wrong.

He hadn't; he'd proved her right instead. A rush of tingles skittered through her chest. She liked that he'd opened up to her. Liked that, in a sense, her instincts were correct.

"So if you *don't* do the interview…" she said in a whisper.

"Then my sister will be furious. She'll feel betrayed, I guess you could say. Also," he added with a humorless laugh, "she says she won't name her baby after me, though I doubt she'd go that far."

Ivy felt her jaw drop a little. "She's naming her baby after you?"

Easton nodded. "Yep. She's thirty weeks along. Well, closer to thirty-one actually, which means that the baby is about as big as a pineapple right now."

Holy Swoonersons! He just kept getting better. "Wow," she said. "That's incredible."

"It was the size of a zucchini last week," he said. "She fills me in on all the developments every time."

Ivy considered that. "There are some pretty big zucchini out there. You should've seen some of the ones we grew in our garden. But I'm sure they mean the little grocery store sized ones," she added.

"Let's hope for *her* sake you're right. She's got another ten weeks to go." Easton flashed her another grin.

Stop swooning, Ivy. She had to have a concussion, that was the only explanation. She couldn't remember the last time she'd been so…so much like a crushing schoolgirl.

But really, his nephew would be named after him? Ivy liked her brothers just fine. She loved them, in fact, but she couldn't imagine naming a child after one in a million years.

"Huh," she managed. But inwardly she was gathering a better picture of him. A strong, protective older brother. Filled with enough honor and goodness that his own sister wanted to name her child after him. The exact type of man she could actually lose her heart to, only to find that he'd never feel the same way.

A streak of sadness crept in as she realized how very true that was.

"I guess what I'm saying is," Easton said softly, as if his mind had carried on the conversation. "I don't really have much of a choice. I agreed to do the interview, and if the storm didn't somehow make it impossible, like I hoped it might..." His face turned chagrined. "Then we may as well just do it." He pinned those dark brown eyes on her. "So, where do you want me?"

CHAPTER 5

Easton shrugged into a fresh tee shirt, a gloomy sense of acceptance pushing its way through his body. After all that he'd been through, he still hadn't earned his way out of the dreaded interview. Not even leaving all of her bags behind had prevented it.

A quick glance over his shoulder said that Ivy was propping her phone on a barstool against a stack of books. She had it aimed at the rocking chair he'd been seated at moments ago, only now it sat before the fire. It was twilight out, and the overhead light that once lit up the space had gone gray, leaving the flames to do the trick.

Ivy sat back onto the stool where she'd positioned it across from the rocking chair, then leaned forward to check the screen. "Okay," she said, her voice much too chipper for the circumstance. "I've got fifty-five percent left on my battery. But nothing drains this phone faster than shooting video, so we'll have to work quick."

Easton nodded and made his way over to the rocking chair. Once his back was to it, he sank back and ran his gaze over the sight before him. He'd be danged if Ivy didn't make those thermals look good. Too good. He'd helped a toddler-sized Chantelle bundle up on cold nights enough times he could've done it in his sleep. There were times, he mused, he practically had. A shudder rocked through him at the memory.

But this...helping secure the waist around Ivy's slender figure, it had him thinking thoughts he had no right to think about a woman he didn't even know. Sure, he'd remained the perfect gentleman on the outside, keeping his hands and eyes from wandering further than necessary. But that mind of his sometimes went rogue.

"So," Ivy said, squinting at her phone for a blink. "I'm pressing record, then I'll start asking the questions."

He gave her another glance over, half expecting her to be holding a cue card. "You've got the questions memorized?"

She nodded. "There are only five."

Relief flooded over him. "Five? Sheesh, why didn't you say so?"

A cute little giggle sounded as she shook her head. There were a lot of things he was starting to like about her. The way she'd encouraged him to speak up about the interview. The way she'd accepted the fact that they were, in fact, stuck. And even the way she sank into his arms after getting smacked by the door, he mused, still shocked it had actually knocked her out. She didn't seem overly concerned about her hair when it was snow-drenched, or the gash in her head that could potentially leave a scar.

She was easy going, he guessed, compared to what he'd

expected anyway. It seemed the two of them had a certain compatibility. Chemistry, even. It would make botching the interview hard, but hopefully not impossible.

"Hey, Ivy?"

She hovered her thumb over the screen. "Yeah?"

"Don't expect this to be…anything special, okay?"

Her face scrunched up in reprove. "Tsk, whatever. You ready?"

No. He nodded anyway.

"Okay, here we go." She straightened back up then, her shoulders tall, her posture poised, as if she'd transformed into some professional reporter in a blink.

His face warmed as he stared into her blue eyes. She was pretty, there'd been no doubt about that from the first moment they'd met. But as he sat across from her now, as she stepped into *her* element, he saw her in a new light. A confident, self-assured light. It was…attractive, he decided. And intimidating.

"So, Easton," she started, "in a competition where twenty-five guys will compete for the attention of just five girls, what do you think will set you apart from the rest?"

Ugh. These were going to be harder than he thought. The last thing he wanted to do was sell himself. He tipped his chin down and gave her a pleading look, willing her to remember how very much he did not want to do this.

Ivy gave him a knowing grin, then nodded encouragingly.

"What makes me different from other guys, huh?" He shrugged, dropped his elbows to his knees, and let out a sigh.

"Oh," she blurted, "I think if you lean down that far you'll get cut off." She tilted sideways to check the screen. "Actually, no. It's…*perfect*." Her cheeks flushed pink.

"I guess what sets me apart is the fact that I don't need a bunch of modern day luxuries to be satisfied. Give me a place to lay my head, a fire to roast my latest kill, and I'm a happy man."

"Your latest kill?" she echoed.

He grinned, hoping the phrase might strike a few nerves with producers.

"You probably already know that our five bachelorettes have already been chosen," she said. "One of those ladies is vegan and a strong animals rights advocate. Would you be willing to change your meat-eating ways if the two of you were to fall in love?"

A hint of amusement struck him as he considered what she asked. "A vegan, eh? I think it's *safer* to say that your scenario is not realistic. It would never happen. She and I wouldn't be compatible, which is fine by me. I'm not one to force my opinions, and I'm not about to change my ways."

He was tempted to leave it there, but the topic was a hot one for him. "I hunt for food, not sport, and I train others to do the same."

"Which leads us to our next question," Ivy said. "Tell us what you do for a living."

This question wouldn't help or hinder him, Easton supposed. He may as well just answer honestly and spread the word about the program. "I'm a co-founder, co-operator of a survival based rehab center for teens and young adults. We provide a nature based experience, no matter the season, where participants can get treatment for a number of addictions or issues, while teaching *physical* life survival skills along the way."

"So you're talking about nights spent in tents and under the stars," she urged.

He nodded. "And days spent out in the elements too, no matter how hot or cold it might get. We make our own fire, catch our own food, and build our own shelter most months too.

"Adding that component—it takes the focus off their own *personal* weakness, whatever it might be, and demonstrates how common our human weakness is when faced with the elements. Learning to overcome those challenges, gaining those essential survival skillsets, it gives the kids a real boost." He willed himself to stop there; he could ramble about that topic all day long.

"That's..." She cleared her throat and sniffed. "That's incredible. What gave you a heart for it?"

Easton gave her a subtle look of reprove. He'd let her first follow-up question slip, about the vegan chick, but this was hitting too close to home.

"My own traumatic childhood," he said, a ring of finality coating his words.

Ivy blanched from the comment, her expression shifting from intrigue to regret. Maybe that would keep her from prying too much. The last thing he wanted to do was get caught in his emotions on camera.

She gave him a slight nod, seeming to acknowledge his intent, then lifted her chin once more. "So your job is to teach them the survival aspect," she said.

He nodded. "Right. We have skilled therapists from diverse fields to address mental illness, addiction, depression, you name it. But my job goes back to the basics. I get people in touch with their caveman side. You never know when it

might come in handy."

He glanced up at her pointedly across the barstool. "Heck, you could be all warm and cozy in your big SUV and suddenly get stuck in a blizzard with no means to save your own hide. If you don't know how to fend and hunt for yourself, you could wind up at the mercy of some heathen." He shot her a wink.

A giggle seemed to get caught in her throat. "Indeed." She rubbed at her arms then, and Easton noticed goosebumps had formed over her skin.

"Are you cold?" he asked, wondering if that were even possible. It was quite warm if you asked him. But Ivy only shook her head.

"No. Thank you." She bit at her lip and glanced down at the phone before lifting those blue eyes back on him. "Tell us about your best relationship experience."

Easton couldn't hide the glare that formed across his brow. Not only did he dislike the question in general, he really disliked the *us* part. It reminded him that this was, in fact, not just a conversation between the two of them. This was still an audition. An audition he very much needed to botch.

"I can't say I've ever had a great," he put up finger quotes "relationship experience. A few are less horrible than the others, if that works."

"In what way?" she pried.

He huffed out a sigh, forcing himself to recall what he liked about his relationship with Luna, one of the counselors who'd spent time at the center. He knew just what set her apart from some of the women he dated. "In the way that she didn't try to change who I am. And I didn't try to change her either. We weren't the same by any means, but we respected what was different about one another, if that makes sense."

A grin pulled at one corner of her mouth. "That does make sense. Thank you."

Easton shifted in his seat, anxious for this to be over. And once it was, would it be very wrong of him to *accidentally* drop her phone into the washing bin? Or fling it into the fire?

"Two final questions, starting with this. They say we often learn about love by the examples set in our youth. In just two sentences, tell us what couple influenced you most, and how you would describe their relationship."

Wow, they were really asking for it, weren't they? But maybe this would work in his favor. Perhaps it was answers like this that would keep him from moving into that final contestant slot.

"My parents," he said holding up a finger for the first sentence. "And to describe their relationship…I can do it in one word." He squared a good hard look at her then, and spit out the only definition that would do it justice. "Toxic."

There, did she want him to elaborate on that topic too?

The crease between her eyes, the sad, softened pull at her brow, said she didn't.

"Last question," she said, her voice nearly defeated. She gulped, cleared her throat, and spoke louder then. "Why should you be one of America's *Looking For Love* bachelors?"

Ah, this was a good one, easy to botch to the hilt.

"I *shouldn't,*" he admitted. "I'm sure there are a whole lot of men out there, dying to find their somebody, whoever that might be. But I'm not one of them. In fact, I don't think I'll be ready for that for a very long time."

Ivy's lips hardened into a straight line. She widened her eyes next and nodded a knowing look toward the camera.

When he did nothing in response, she huffed out a breath. "Then why did you audition? And why agree to the interview?"

He guessed she was forced to ask the question, since she already knew the answer. This time he wouldn't reveal the truth. Instead, he'd offer something else. "I guess I just changed my mind," he said, tightening his jaw to show he was done.

It felt as if they were in a standoff, the way she held his gaze and stared him down while he did the same, unabashed.

"Is that all of your questions?" he urged, hoping to call an end to it once and for all.

Ivy reached for the phone and snatched if off the barstool. "Yes," she said, tapping the screen with her thumb. "That's all." Irritation poured off her tone. Her frustration was evident in her quick and angry movement as well. She thumped at the screen some more before pressing a small button alongside to shut off the device. At once she tugged at the neck of her shirt and wedged the phone in what he could only assume was her bra.

"I can put that over here on the table if you don't want to—"

"It's fine," she spat, grabbing the books off the barstool and putting them back where she'd gotten them.

He watched as she stomped back to the stool, snatched it off the floor, and hurried it back where it had been as well.

"Hey, some people's past isn't very pretty," he defended. "What, did you want me to make up some pretty little tale?"

"No, Easton. It's fine."

But it wasn't fine. And why had he liked the way she called him by his name? As if she were already, after just half of a day, so familiar with him?

His stomach growled in the quiet pause, causing him to realize how long it had been since he'd eaten. And how long it must have been since she'd eaten too.

"Are you hungry?" he asked.

"No," she spat, but then added to it. "Maybe." She moved back to her bench, turned it to face the fire instead of him, and plunked down onto it.

Easton glanced down at her sock-covered feet, a thick wool pair he'd leant her. Ivy's leg bounced restlessly as she stared into the fire, her jaw visibly set into a tight clench.

Helplessness quickly gave way to irritation of his own. This was the reason he didn't want a relationship. He didn't like playing games. Having to guess at what the other was thinking. Stewing over every imagined possibility as if—

"I don't know which parts were true and which parts weren't," Ivy blurted, shooting to a sudden stand. "*That's* why I'm frustrated."

...Or maybe she *wasn't* going to make him guess after all. He followed her movement with his eyes, from one side of the yurt to the next as she paced back and forth. "I get that you didn't want to do this, but this is my career, you know? I'm supposed to push and pry and get all the information I can and you...you made that impossible!"

Easton tipped his head. "How?"

She paused mid-stride and darted a glare at him. "By...by giving me one-word answers that brought my questions to a screeching halt."

"Did you want me to lie?"

"I figured you already *were* lying since you admitted that being on the show was the last thing you'd ever want to do."

"It *is*," he assured, coming to a stand as well.

"So what parts were true and what parts weren't?"

He sifted back through the questions. "Almost all of it was true."

"*Almost?* You made a mockery out of the whole thing."

"How did I make a mockery out of it?" he asked, throwing his hands up.

"And believe it or not," she continued, "there's big money in this industry. It's nothing to turn your nose up at."

"Just because there's money in it doesn't make it right."

"There's nothing *wrong* with it either, Easton. It's a matchmaking show, get it? Most people have a very hard time finding their match. And thanks to a long list of Marsha Langston's dating shows—many of which I've played a part in—dozens of people have found the love of their lives. You can't just dismiss that."

A small knot formed in his gut as he realized something very surprising. She was passionate about this. Passionate about people finding love.

He shook his head, fighting back the words in his mind. *Too bad you can't take a glimpse into the future to see what comes after those happily ever afters you think exist.* Or perhaps, he thought, a level of envy washing over him, perhaps it was better if she never did. Not everyone needed to become as jaded and pessimistic as he was. In fact, he mused as she carried on, it would be a shame if she did.

"...And that doesn't even include the number of contestants

who *didn't* make it to the end but still found love," she was saying. "Since it's all aired on TV, most contestants come out with a pretty big fan base, resulting in hundreds of marriages in the last eight years."

He'd resigned himself to leave the first rebuttal alone, but another one rose in its place. One he couldn't ignore as easily. "Well, if it's so great, Ivy, why don't *you* enter?"

Her mouth went from poised to pursed in a blink. "Because I don't *want* to," she spat.

The adamant tone she'd slapped onto her statement made him wonder if she, in fact, had her own jaded edge. He held her gaze for a blink, wanting very badly to know her inner thoughts. The thoughts she refused to speak aloud.

"You don't *want* to?" he echoed.

"No."

"Neither do I," he assured.

Her eyes widened before she narrowed them into a seething glare. "You're impossible." With that, she pushed past him, bumping his shoulder with her folded arms.

He glanced behind him to see her stand before the fire. Seconds ago, while she was speaking with all that passion and flare, every limb was tightly locked into place. But now, as she let out a heavy sigh, all those limbs went limp. Her shoulders and knees slouching as if she'd aged a hundred years after their conversation. She was...defending something, he felt. But what?

Guilt rumbled low in his gut. She was right. He *was* impossible. The trouble was, he wasn't sure how to make it right. He recalled her frantic insistence when he brought her to the yurt. She'd been determined to do the interview and go catch her flight. The poor woman was down in more ways than one, and Easton was only adding to it.

His urge to argue his points fell away. He walked over to the bench she stood beside and took a seat on the end farthest from her.

"I'm sorry," he said, gaze fixed on the fire.

"You are?" She turned to look at him, searching his face for a blink.

"Yes," he said.

She took hold of her phone once more, pressed the power button, then looked up at him in question. "Okay, then I need you to do one last thing."

He fought back an eye roll. "What?"

She tapped the phone screen, swiped her thumb across it, and handed it over. "Sign the contract," she said. "It says that the station can use this interview to determine whether you move on to the next round or not. And that, if you do, you agree to show up."

Easton groaned as he took hold of the device. His inner voice was screaming—*don't sign anything. You'll be locked in for sure.*

"If I don't sign it?" he asked, testing.

Ivy gave him a warning glare. "Then it's the same thing as refusing the interview. You wouldn't be doing what you promised your sister you'd do."

He figured that. So it was inevitable. He stared at the screen, his insides starting some sort of revolt. "Fine," he managed. "I just sign this line with my finger?"

"Yes," she instructed. "It will ask for your thumbprint too, to verify that you're the one who signed it, in case you tried to deny it later."

Geeze. "I wouldn't." He wasn't a liar.

"Then we're good."

Easton let out a defeated huff and squiggled his name across the screen. "There," he said, attempting to hand it back.

Ivy pulled her hand away like the phone might burn her. "The thumb print?" she prompted.

"Oh yeah." Easton rested his thumb in place and felt it pulse just beneath. A small beep sounded as a green checkmark filled the screen. *Done.* As in, too late to turn back now. That fact seemed to prod at parts of his insides. His muscles went tight. If only he hadn't made that stupid bet.

But he couldn't dwell on it forever. His stomach growled once more, reminding him of what he'd planned to do a moment ago.

"Now then," he said, a bit relieved that was out of the way. "Let's see what we can do about food, and maybe we'll both be in a better state to talk this out. Sound good?"

She bit at her lip. "When you say *see what we can do about food..."*

"I mean send you into the storm with a bow and arrow," he finished for her.

She laughed over her response. "Perfect."

CHAPTER 6

Ivy pulled a set of small, bamboo spoons from the water bin and rested them on the table beside the soup tins. It was warm enough that they should dry off quickly, as Easton promised.

"So you're telling me that, even though you were with two brothers *and* an older sister, *you* were the one to put the worm on the hook?" Easton's eyes were wide with wonder.

"I *really* was the one. They were all too grossed out by it." She let out a chuckle as he shook his head.

"So what happened once you caught the fish? Who took care of that part?"

For a split second she contemplated not answering that question, but her curiosity won out; she *had* to see his reaction to it. "We never caught anything."

"Whoa, whoa, whoa," he said, putting his hands out before him. "You had a pond with fish in it right next to your house."

"Yep."

"And all of this top of the line fishing gear…" he added.

Ivy gave him a nod. "Uh, huh."

"And yet you never once caught a fish?"

"Never once."

"Wow."

She chuckled, appreciating his response.

"It almost *hurts* to hear that," he admitted. "We would have starved if I hadn't known how to fish. Makes me glad I do what I do."

"I'm sure it does." She gestured to the wash bin. "Should we dump this out or just leave it here?"

"Leave it," he said with the jerk of his head. "Let's come over by the fire." Easton led the way, snatching a jar of sorts from his backpack and heading over. He scooted the bench toward the wall before resting the big bear rug in front of the fireplace once more.

"Why don't you grab those spoons over there. I've got some dessert for us."

"Dessert?" Her brows lifted as she grabbed the wooden spoons off the table and headed over to join him.

"I've got cinnamon rolls too," he said, "but I figure we should save them."

Ivy lowered herself onto the rug, enjoying the mood in the air. They'd built a level of camaraderie over dinner, and even flirted a bit with the sparks of chemistry she'd noticed earlier that day. She wouldn't admit it any time soon, but Ivy had loved hearing Easton say that he didn't want to go on the show.

She didn't *want* him going on the show either. Or at least, the dreamer inside her didn't want that. The part that believed —despite his disinterest in *Looking For Love*—that he might want to find love outside of that setting. Maybe he'd even want to find love with her beside the crackling fire and the blustering storm outside.

It was ideas like those that brought her back to more realistic thoughts. Ones that said a relationship between the two of them would probably never work out. Which, Ivy reminded herself, was fine by her; she wasn't ready to start dating again.

It was amazing, the odd sense of peace she felt each time she clung onto that no-dating rule of hers. All fear, insecurities, and doubts took flight. Sadly, the determination also wiped out things like hope, potential, and delicious anticipation. Something she'd been enjoying just seconds ago.

Was it really worth the trade off?

"You ready to give these things a try?" Easton asked, pulling her out of her musings. He twisted the lid off the jar with a pop and gave it a whiff. "Whoa," he cried with the shake of his head. "A few of these should keep us warm through the night."

Ivy tilted her head, unsure of what he meant. It looked like a regular old jar of peaches like her mom canned every year. "What kind of peaches *are* they?" she ventured, handing over one of the spoons.

Easton, who'd been eyeing the jar, lifted his gaze to meet hers. His brow arched, and a grin pulled at one side of his lips. "Moonshine."

"Ah," she said with the tip of her head. "Like where they add homemade liquor or something?"

"Yep." He dug his spoon into the jar and scooped up one of the peaches. They'd been cut in half, then cut in half again, leaving them in quarters. "Go ahead," he urged. "We'll cheers with our spoons."

A laugh snuck up her throat. "Okay." She eyed the jar warily, wondering how good a peach soaked in moonshine could actually be. She stuck her spoon in, scored a peach for herself, and lifted it from the jar's wide rim.

A look of triumph spread over Easton's face as he lifted his spoon toward hers. "Cheers," he bellowed.

"Cheers," she said through another laugh. Ivy brought it to her mouth quickly, determined to eat it without gagging. She chewed a few times, swallowed it down, and paused to assess the flavors left on her tongue. There was a strong taste that didn't belong to a peach—that was the moonshine. But she tasted the tangy sweetness of the peach as well.

"That's not bad," she decided, hovering her spoon over the rim once more. She scooped up another thick slice and looked at him. "You're eating more too, aren't you?"

He nodded. "Definitely. But I have to warn you, my neighbor Jerry—he's the one who makes them—goes *heavy* on the liquor."

Ivy rarely ever drank, but how much damage could bottled fruit do? "Did you know that we've got between two to four *thousand* taste buds?"

"No," Easton said.

"We do. And they're not all just on the tongue either. Some are at the back of your throat, your esophagus, your nose..."

He grinned. "That's awesome."

"I'm a fun fact geek," she warned, wondering if she should resist the urge to share what came to her mind.

"So am I. Did you know the tongue is made up of like eight muscles, all interwoven together?" he asked, proving his point.

"The structure's similar to an elephant's trunk or even an octopus's tentacle."

He wasn't kidding. "I've never known a guy who could spout fun facts like me." In an odd way, it made Ivy feel…safe to be herself.

"Chantelle says I store up useless but fascinating knowledge," Easton said. "It drives her crazy."

"It drives *my* family crazy too," Ivy assured.

They kept their eyes locked on one another, their connection deepening in the quiet space.

Until Easton spoke up. "Did you know that eyes contain the fastest—"

"Muscles in the human body?" she finished for him. "They don't say *blink of an eye* for nothing."

The two burst into laughter at once.

"I think I've met my match," he said with an appraising nod.

They ate a few more peaches before Ivy spoke up again. "Wow, I've never met a fellow fact geek. In the time we spend together, we're going to nearly double one another's useless data bank. Then we'll *really* drive our families crazy."

Easton laughed out loud, the genuine sound of it making her feel at home somehow. "That calls for another cheers, I think." He steadied his spoon while Ivy readied hers.

"I think you're right," she said, lifting it to clank it against his. She ate that peach, and a few more, realizing that, despite Easton's flawless appearance, Ivy felt more at ease with him than she'd felt with a man in a very long time. A man she was attracted to, anyway.

"I'm impressed that a *guy* made these," she said between bites. "I pictured some old lady in an apron."

"Jerry's great," Easton said. "He's retired, makes and delivers them every Christmas. Of course, his kids took his license from him over the summer—guess he was getting dangerous out on the roads—so I helped him deliver them this time."

Ivy gulped down the next peach as a new and welcome warmth stirred in her heart. "That's so sweet of you."

Easton only shrugged. "He lives right next door. And I don't mind helping the guy out when he needs it." He seemed to think about that for a bit before adding, "Heck, it's only a matter of time before I'll need that kind of help too."

Ivy nodded. "Guess that's true for all of us. I dread the day we have to tell one of my parents that they shouldn't be driving anymore."

Easton looked away quickly, then dropped his gaze to the jar. "Yeah," he offered. "That reminds me, I'm sorry you'll have to miss your family party. Sounds like it's really important to you."

"Thank you," she said, but inwardly she was thinking back on what he'd shared during the interview. That his childhood was traumatic. She tied that piece of his past with another he'd shared—of how he'd wrapped his baby sister up in his old thermals at night to keep her warm. A shiver rocked through her. How was it that someone could be raised so...poorly yet turn out so good?

She wanted to ask him that very thing. Instead, Ivy followed his spoon into the jar and snatched the slice he'd scored right off the scooped surface. "That one looks *good,*" she said with a laugh.

"*Hey,*" Easton chuckled. "I picked that one because it looked the best."

She couldn't help but giggle some more. The mood was just so...light suddenly. And Easton was so warm and welcoming and wonderful. "Here," she said, feeling playful now. She straightened her arm toward him. "Open up and I'll feed you. *But,*" she stipulated, "you have to do the same with me next."

He backed away slightly, eyeing her for a blink. "Okay." He sounded wary, which only made Ivy laugh some more. This was a good night. As horrible as it had begun and as deadly as her predicament had been, this moment with Easton by the fire felt like magic.

She kept her gaze fixed on his lips as he ate the peach off her spoon and wiped his mouth.

"Mmm," he rumbled from low in his throat. "It's *your* turn." The way he said it, with the lift of that brow and the gleam in his eye, felt more like a warning.

"You're going to do it nicely, like I did, right?" she cautioned. "This isn't that whole cake at a wedding thing where they shove food in each other's faces."

"I hate that tradition," he said, scooping a peach from the jar. "Open up."

A spurt of reluctance gripped hold of her as he lifted the spoon. "You didn't agree with me yet."

"Yes I did," he said, steadying the spoon as he straightened his arm toward her.

Ivy backed away from it and shook her head. "Just say you'll give it to me nicely like I did you." Her words might have been coated in laughter, but she'd meant them all the same.

He huffed out an exhausted breath.

"Please," she urged, forcing her lips into a pout.

Easton squared a serious look at her. "Ivy?"

She loved the sound of her name in his raspy voice. "Yes," she urged.

"I hereby promise to deliver this moonshine peach gently into that pretty little mouth of yours."

Her heart went into some sort of spasm. Chills rushed over her arm and legs and possibly everything else too. "Okay." She let out a shaky breath, leaned toward him, and opened up.

He spooned the slice into her mouth just as he'd said, but a drop of juice still spilled down her lip. Before she could catch it herself, Easton slid his thumb along her lower lip. She watched in surprise as he licked it off. "Mmmm," he rasped. "I was wrong."

She gulped. "Wrong about what?"

"About that other slice being the best." He nodded in her direction. "I'm using all two to four thousand taste buds, and I have to say that *that* one was the tastiest yet."

CHAPTER 7

Perhaps breaking out the moonshine peaches wasn't such a good idea after all. Easton had realized, during the whole feeding each other encounter, that the liquor was already hitting her.

He'd done the responsible thing—sealed up the jar at its halfway point and set it away from them, but the effects hadn't begun to wear off. Normally, that might not be a problem. Because normally, women didn't have this kind of effect on him.

Ivy Ingles was different. Every time he expected one thing, she did another. Even now, as she sat before the fire, those loose locks of golden hair framing her pretty face in the firelight, she was grinning from ear to ear. Not pouting about being stuck in a blizzard. Not carrying a grudge about the crappy interview.

He mused over their recent conversation. She'd asked more about his job, told him more about hers. All the while, her words were laced with a slur, courtesy of the moonshine.

He let out a sigh as he watched the way she trailed her fingers over the bearskin rug, her brow slightly furrowing in thought. Suddenly she scooted closer to him, and not very slyly either.

The two might very well look like they were in a couple's yoga class, legs crossed beneath them while facing each other, a foot-space of distance lying between them. That is, until she moved in again. Her knees brushed against his, sending sprouts of desire to take root. At least their folded legs kept them from getting any closer than this.

"Hi," she said with a grin.

He couldn't help but chuckle under his breath as he replied. "Hi."

She leaned forward then, releasing a breathy sigh as she set her hand over his where they rested in his lap.

Whoa. The warmth of her was everywhere. It felt nice having her so close.

"Thanks again for saving me today," she said softly.

Easton gave her a nod. "You're welcome."

"I feel really..." She paused, her blue eyes gleaming with mischief. "...*warm* toward you right now."

Okay, now she *really* sounded drunk. And after what—a few measly peach slices? *Lightweight.*

Still, heat stirred low in his belly. Her closeness, her comment, the way she was looking at him—all of it had him thinking of that tempting mouth of hers. Of how, when the peach juice dripped down her lip and he'd gotten a taste of it, he'd wanted to rush in for a taste of her lips too. Even now, the urge was as constant and prodding as the beat of his heart.

He gulped, forcing his mind someplace else as the belly heat stirred once more. "We should get a sleeping bag set up for you," he said.

But Ivy moved her hand to his bicep, urging him to stay put. He ran his gaze over her face, enjoying the way the firelight complimented her skin. "I'm having some thoughts inside," she admitted.

Oh, no. Where was his canteen when he needed it? She was dehydrated for sure—that would explain the strong reaction.

"Why don't you tell me about your *thoughts* when you wake up?"

"Of what it would be like to kiss you," she finished.

Easton's pulse spiked. "I think that's the moonshine talking," he forced himself to say. "You don't drink often, do you?"

"No," she admitted.

Neither did Easton, but he wasn't affected the way she was. Of course, Ivy was considerably smaller than him.

"Listen, Ivy. I might be having similar…thoughts, but—"

A huge smile took over her face, distracting him from what he'd planned to say. Dang, she was cute. And she was nudging impossibly closer even still, as if what he'd said was an invitation.

"But," he added, resting a hand over her grip on his bicep.

"You're muscles are really strong," she said.

He grinned and gave her small hand a squeeze before guiding it back toward her own lap. "But…" he started again. "I don't think it's a good idea." The words hovered in the air for a bit, like unwelcome insects at a picnic.

"Why not?" She blinked wide eyes at him, looking very childlike suddenly. It helped—in a sense—keep him from taking advantage of the moment. She wasn't exactly herself right now. But Easton *was* and he needed to tell her the truth.

"Because I...I have a hard time believing in love." He sighed, deflating as the truth of his reply took him back to reality in a blink. "I see it go bad so often that...that I've decided it's not worth the risk."

She blanched. "You don't believe in love?"

He thought about his sister and Tim. About how the two of them seemed to have found something truly special. With them, he at least had hope that they wouldn't end up like most couples did—miserable in the wake of so much hurt and destruction, their kids often taking the brunt.

"For some people, I think it works," he admitted. "For the lucky ones. But something tells me that I'll never be that lucky."

A crease formed between her eyes. "I say things like that too. I say that I don't want to date right now because I'm busy with work and I want to get my promotion and blah, blah, blah, but really I'm just scared of getting my heart broken again."

Another admission, courtesy of the moonshine. Yet somehow it struck a chord. A chord that said, when it came down to it, Easton was scared of that very thing. Terrified, actually.

His heart picked up its pace then, escalating to a sudden restless racing that had him itching to take flight.

"I think we should get some sleep now," he said, shooting to a stand and heading toward the sleeping bags.

Wait, wrong direction. He spun in place, bolted toward the cabinet, and secured one bag and two pillows.

"We're going to share?" Ivy asked, coming to a stand as he neared.

Her question earned a genuine laugh, dark as it might be. That was all he needed, a night of lying close beside her, inhaling the sweet scent of her hair while she wrapped her fingers around his arm once more.

What would possibly stop him from curling up even closer? Cupping the lovely curve of her waist and nuzzling into the bend of her shoulder, her neck just a breath space away from his mouth…

"Nope," he assured. "I've got a blanket in my pack. The sleeping bags, with all this heat from the fire, would be too warm for me."

"Oh yeah, because you're so much hotter." This time the comment was missing the element of humor. It sounded almost…accusing. She was upset with him, he realized, for not kissing her. Well, she'd thank him in the morning.

"Not hotter, Ivy. Warmer."

He was quick to unroll her bag, prop a pillow at the top, and unzip the side. All the while his head was spinning with the ideas that her *sharing a sleeping bag* question had forced into his mind.

"You're the hot one of the two of us, remember?" he said with a wink. He'd been going for playful, but the tone was all wrong. Who cared? He just needed to get this woman in her own bag and back far, far away.

"Here," he said, giving the bag a pat. "Climb in and I'll tend to the fire."

Please, Ivy. Just do what I asked.

Or ask me to kiss you again. Just once, and this time I will.

He cleared his throat, eyes fixed on her as she rather crawled over to the bag, that beautiful pout in place. "Okay..." She dragged out the word and put an edge on it.

A wave of relief poured over him, which was good. It showed he had some decency left in him still. But then a flood of disappointment crashed in, stronger than the fleeting relief. Perhaps he wasn't so decent after all.

Easton spent a longer time tending to the fire than necessary, keenly listening, all the while, to the pace of Ivy's breath. Only once it was slow and steady did he step away, snatch his own blanket from the pack, and park in front of the door. The only kiss he'd be sharing with Ivy that night would be in his dreams.

CHAPTER 8

The presents were wrapped and waiting beneath her tree. Ivy had one for everyone. Her brothers, her sister, and the in-laws too. Mom and Dad would love their new coffee maker; Mom because it would make those fancy cappuccinos she was always blowing her money on, and Dad because it would stop Mom from blowing her money on them.

She shifted from one shoulder to the next, her thoughts drifting dreamily to the items she'd bought for the nieces and nephews. She could see them now, tearing the wrapping off the gifts before a crackling fire.

Her eyes shot open. *I'm in a cave. With Easton.*

She sat up quickly, her head throbbing in response, and glanced about the space. A yurt, she reminded herself.

"How'd you sleep, Sunshine?" She spun to see him seated beside the table on the rocking chair, a book in his hand.

It had gotten lighter, but it wasn't the kind of light that said there was sun outside. "Is the storm still going?" she asked.

Easton nodded. "It's a mean one." A gust of wind whistled throughout the structure to prove the point.

Ivy's mind shot back to her previous musings, causing a sudden burst of panic to push through her. "My family," she blurted. "They'll be worried sick if they don't hear from me today. Do you think there's any way we can tell them I'm okay?"

Easton came to a stand, his brow furrowing while he scratched at his jaw. His short facial hair looked thicker this morning. "It's possible," he said while heading toward the fire, "that, if the storm lets up a bit, I could make my way close enough to the lodge to send a text." He tossed a thumb over his shoulder.

"I can go with you," she said, hating the idea of getting stranded there without him. "How far is it?"

"On foot, it's a ways out there for sure. We've got a few pair of snow shoes," he said. "But you'll get your clothes all drenched again." He nodded toward her. "Which means you'll end up right back in my thermals."

Ivy glanced down to see that the neck of his top had slid down her shoulder again. She hiked it back into place and came to a stand, hope sprouting in her chest as she realized what he was saying. "You'll let me come then?"

He gulped. "I'd probably be faster without you," he said more to himself.

"Thanks a lot."

"You know what I mean," he said with a shrug. "Get yourself a cinnamon roll and I'll take a look outside. Who knows, maybe we'll be able to check the forecast and see if there's been any change. If it clears up, and if the airport is opening flights again, maybe we can get you home in time for your party after all."

Ivy forced herself to nod. "That would be *awesome.*" But inwardly, she'd grown attached to the idea of spending another day with Easton. There was chemistry between them, she was sure of it. And another day spent together, heck, that might be all they needed to discover there really was something there.

No, Ivy. You don't want to get hurt again. One look at the mass of physical perfection by the fireplace said it all. Easton could have any woman he wanted, but he'd chosen to be alone. The thought gave her pause; he'd said that last night, hadn't he? That he didn't believe in love. How sad.

She searched through her memories some more. She'd been pretty affected by the moonshine peaches, Ivy remembered that much. Oh, and he'd fed her a peach and licked his thumb after catching a drop of juice from her lip. She'd wanted him to kiss her and... A dose of embarrassed heat pooled into her face. Had she said it aloud? That she wanted to kiss him?

"You going to eat?" Easton asked, breaking into her thoughts.

"Yes." Ivy stretched and yawned, hoping to appear natural as her mind scoured the events she could recall. At last, she came up empty. Whether she'd voiced that desire or not, there was nothing she could do now to change it.

Best to simply leave it in the past and focus on today. It would also be best, she realized as Easton cracked open the door to survey the storm, if she was somehow able to catch a flight out before the day was through. She could get the interview to Marsha, have the evening—or at least Christmas Day—with her family, and leave thoughts of Easton Sparks behind her.

A wry chuckle threatened to sneak up her throat at the

thought alone. Who was she kidding? Once Marsha got her hands on that interview—as imperfect as Ivy had once thought that it was—she'd want Easton on the show all the more. He'd be the Darcy of the bunch. The handsome brooder with a difficult past.

Jealousy twisted in the center of her gut. The five bachelorettes would be all over him. The vegan would probably be eating bacon off his fork by the time the show was through.

Who cared? He didn't belong to her, and if he had it his way, he wouldn't belong to anyone. Let the brave bachelorettes lose their hearts to him one by one. Ivy would remain nicely within her no-dating boundaries, safe from the wrath.

Ivy waited for that conviction to lend the calming effect it usually did. Waited while sitting at the table and biting into the cinnamon roll he'd set out for her. Yet, even as she ate, finishing the entire roll in just a few bites, the calm never came. This time, all she could feel was the heavy lack of hope.

Ivy hurried through the open door as the storm nearly pushed her through the entrance. A slate of snow cased her at either side, making her all the more anxious to step into the warmth.

Easton hurried in behind her and shoved the door closed with his elbow. He jiggled the handle next, then secured the lock and turned to look at her. "There," he said. "If you do *that*, it won't slam back open and smack you upside the head."

"Good to know," she said. "Speaking of which, I wonder how my head's doing?"

Easton reached over and tugged the wool hat—something he'd leant her—right off her head.

Ivy's hand shot to her static-ridden hair. "Hey..."

He grinned. "This is a good look for you." But then he shifted his gaze to her bandage and gently traced along the sides. "I'll take a look at it once we're dried off. For now, let's get out of these snow shoes."

Ivy hobbled over to the bench. She'd gotten the hang of walking over the snow with the shoes, but moving about the yurt was a different story. "I feel like Big Foot," she said with a laugh.

"Except that you're just the opposite," Easton teased. "You're little foot."

She giggled. "And *you're* Big Foot?"

"Definitely," he admitted.

Quiet took over the space as they stepped out of their snowshoes, then out of their other boots next. Easton had let the fire die down, leaving nothing but embers in the fireplace.

"You go ahead and change first," he urged, "and I'll get the fire going again." He turned his back to her then, and Ivy felt that inner spot of warmth trying to resurface. He really was a great guy, wasn't he? Decent and good.

"Thanks," she said, hurrying over to his bag where she placed the folded clothes. "And thanks for making the trek out there to the lodge. I can't believe how lucky we got that the wind wasn't blowing on the way there. With as strong as it was on the way back, practically pushing us, I can't imagine fighting against that the whole time."

"Yeah," Easton agreed. "I'd have had to take you back and go myself."

She shook her head. "You keep saying stuff like that."

"Only because it's true."

A chuckle snuck out. "Whatever." Ivy had already switched out of her shirt and was moving on to her pants. She couldn't help but glance over her shoulder before unbuttoning her jeans.

Just as she'd guessed, Easton's gaze was trained directly on the fire as he propped the fresh logs in place.

Her mind shot back to their moments outside the lodge. The mere recollection caused her heart to race. She'd done something she hadn't planned to do, which was to try and upload the footage of Easton to the station's i-cloud where she had her own private file. She'd done the same with his signed contract too. Sure, Nancy could access the folder if she wanted, but there would be no need. Once Ivy got back she could edit the interview and forward it, along with the contract, on to Marsha.

The thought came to her, as it had several times before, that she could choose *not* to forward it on as well. Her motives behind that idea were purely selfish, not to mention foolish. But she did like knowing it was an option. Especially considering that when Easton checked the weather report, round two of the storm, which had started once they were heading back, would last longer than round one. They may even be stuck here over Christmas.

Ivy traded her own socks and shoes for Easton's thick, wool socks as she considered their snowy excursion. While sending the data to her backup storage, she'd decided *not to* tell Easton what she was doing. Not that it should matter. Still, she'd risked sucking even more of her battery with the energy it took to do so, leaving her with a measly twelve percent.

But that was okay, she realized. Easton was a trained professional; there was no one better to be snowed-in with than him. In more ways than one, she mused, recalling the chiseled state of his bare chest. The enticing banter they'd shared since she arrived. Still, Ivy decided as she walked toward the rod propped close to the fire, Easton close by her side, it'd be best if she steered clear of the moonshine tonight.

CHAPTER 9

Laughter filled the glowing yurt all the way up to the domed rooftop, his mingled with hers, and Easton was enjoying every moment of it. The best part about it was that neither had even touched the spiked peaches. The buzz in the air was all natural, all consuming and, he was quite certain, addictive too.

The day had given way to night once more, the hours filled with easy conversation, puzzles and games, and stories of Christmas Eves past—Ivy's, not his.

"So your dad dodges five lanes of heavy traffic in a cop car, all to propose to your mother at Grand Park?"

"Yep. He was quite the romantic."

"Guess I should be on my best behavior," he realized. "Spending late nights with the sheriff's daughter."

She giggled. "He's not the sheriff anymore, but he still works for the department, and he *still* has a patrol car."

"Good. He can help out the guy who proposes to *you,*" Easton said.

"Right."

A sting of jealousy sneaked in at the thought. Easton ignored it.

"I tell you," Ivy said with a sigh, "growing up in a big family, we really did have a whole lot of fun."

"It sure sounds like it." Easton enjoyed the way her blue eyes lit up as she talked about her terrifying encounter with a mall Santa, or the time she and her siblings snuck into the closet and peeked at their presents early one year. Ivy had, without even knowing it, managed to alter his perspective. One that had been etched in stone until now.

"I have to tell you," he said, "when I see life through your eyes, the way your childhood was, it gives me hope. What you had, it's very different from my own experience. It's a stark contrast from the life many of the kids who come through here have known as well. That's why it's been easy to convince myself that happy families don't really exist."

Ivy tipped her head, her expression turning thoughtful now. "Yes, I've been fortunate. Of course, coming from a big family has its downsides."

"Like what?" he wondered.

"Being the youngest," she started, "I felt I was miles behind everyone, you know? I was barely starting to learn one thing, and all of my siblings were mastering bigger, more impressive feats. It just seemed like no matter what I did, I couldn't get them to notice or..." She dropped off there and shook her head. "It's a stupid complaint. In comparison to what other people deal with..."

Other people. As in *him*. She was recalling their interview, no doubt. "Comparison doesn't make what you went through irrelevant, Ivy. Compared to kids with violent parents, my life was a walk in the park. You see?"

She nodded, but the conflicted pull at her brow remained.

"Go ahead," he urged. "Believe it or not, this type of thing helps with my job. I'm not one of the therapists, obviously, just a survival specialist. But sometimes, for that very reason, the kids open up to me all the more. I've had a lot of them say they feel invisible next to their high-achieving siblings. People handle that in different ways," he explained. "Many simply get into trouble to get the attention they want."

How true that was. One kid in particular came to mind. A bright young man named Aaron. He'd been given every opportunity in the world to achieve greatness, but the combination of hurt, jealousy, and the need to be seen resulted in a deadly stream of behavior that almost killed him.

"I guess that's true," she said, reluctant to give herself any credit. "In my case, it's made me determined to achieve greatness. At first, that greatness was getting good grades. Then it was getting a job with Channel 13. Once I achieved that, my goal was to work my way up to a direct position with Marsha Langston, the network's top reality TV producer, which is what I do now. But since none of those accomplishments have impressed anyone a whole lot, I'm aiming to become her number *one* assistant, so..."

Easton realized something as she dropped off there and nodded her head. "You don't enjoy your job?" he asked.

Her mouth snapped open, but nothing came out. She pinched her lips together for a blink, seeming to consider it. "I liked it better when I didn't feel like I was competing for more all the time," she finally said. "But there are still things I like about it."

"Like what?" he asked.

"The interview part has always been my favorite," she said without hesitation. "I love getting to know people. Having them open up about their life. Of course, if I get the promotion I'm going for, I won't do many of those any more."

He held her gaze for a blink, then reached out to slide a finger along her cheek. "Sounds like you might want to reconsider the position."

She nodded, but stayed quiet, biting at her lip in contemplation. "Maybe." A wry laugh slipped from her lips. "You ever allow volunteers at this place?"

Her question surprised and pleased him all at once. "Yes," he said. "We rely on them, in fact. You have to pass a background check, of course. But we have a lot of volunteers come through here."

"I think it'd be rewarding work," she said. "You get to play a part in changing lives, at a crucial time too. It's neat. Admirable."

"I'm fortunate," he agreed. "And for future reference, if you *do* decide to volunteer here, I've got a few words of wisdom. First, wear boots without those little heels in back."

She laughed. "Right."

"And second, steer clear of the moonshine peaches." He winked at her. "You get enough of those things in the two of us, and we might just wake up in the same sleeping bag."

Her face flushed red. "Are you saying that's a *bad* thing?" she teased, causing his face to heat up next. His belly roared with heat as well.

"Not from my perspective," he said through a chuckle.

She sighed through a laugh of her own, then fixed her gaze on him. "You don't have to talk about it if you'd rather not," she said, "but you mentioned that your childhood was…"

Easton took the cue. "Traumatic, yes. And I don't mind. To give you the gist without all the dreary details, we grew up in a crack house, if you can call it a house. It was this run down little place next to the train tracks. A total dump. Torn carpet, damaged furniture, bare cupboards a lot of the time. At one point, we were missing a wall…"

"A wall?" she echoed.

He nodded, recalling the state of it as he fixed his gaze on the fire. "Not an inside wall either. My dad was on a bender, and he rammed his truck right through the back of the house where our bedroom was. He hung a tarp over the hole, supported it along the rain gutter with a two-by-four, and promised to fix it before the winter came, but that never happened.

"For the entire season, I used my mattress to help block out the cold. During that time, my sister and I, we slept on a heap of my mom's old clothes in the closet. It's a wonder that no one discovered the conditions we were being raised in."

A shiver rocked through him. "Of course, my dad warned that if I ever told anyone about what our home life was like, they'd tear me and Chantelle apart and put us in different homes. He knew that was my one weak spot. I swear to you, I *lived* to protect her."

Easton pulled his gaze off the fire in time to see Ivy smear tears off her cheeks. She exhaled a breath through pursed lips, seeming to fight back further tears. He almost hated planting such an image in her head. Of course, she lived in the same world he did; she had to know childhoods like his existed. But she likely hadn't known someone who'd experienced such a life firsthand. Even that was encouraging, if he were honest.

"You told me that you have a hard time believing in love," Ivy said with a sniff.

She remembered that, did she? "Sadly, yes."

"But your sister doesn't share that outlook."

He shook his head. "No, but that's a *good* thing. If she was the way I am, she wouldn't have Tim, and she wouldn't be expecting a baby who's probably going to be one of the coolest humans ever born." Easton smiled. He might not have met his nephew yet, but already the little guy owned a big piece of his heart.

"Do you think that *you're* the reason she sees things in a different light?" Ivy asked.

"What do you mean?"

"Her experience. You might have been raised by the same people in the same house, but her experience was different from yours, because she had *you* looking out for her."

Whoa. That was insightful. Impactful too.

A burst of warmth bloomed in his chest. Easton hadn't thought of it that way before. *No.* People were designed differently right from the start. And Chantelle, she'd always been more optimistic and carefree.

But what if he'd been the reason for that?

As hesitant as he was to take any credit, Ivy's observation

had a ring of truth. A truth that was burrowing deeper into his heart even still.

"I like that idea," he admitted under his breath. Now *his* eyes were welling with tears. He blinked them back quickly and cleared his throat. "I was shooting for keeping her alive." He laughed. "And distracting her enough that she didn't know how bad things really were."

"You must have done a good job at it."

"Thank you." For a reason he couldn't explain, Easton felt lighter suddenly. As if a giant burden had been lifted right off his shoulders. A burden he hadn't even known was there.

"So your sister wants you to find someone," Ivy said. "Is *this* —enrolling you in the *Looking For Love* show—her first attempt to get you dating?"

If only. Easton shook his head. "Not even close. She's set me up on dates, created profiles for me on dating sites, the works."

Ivy grinned. "I bet she's pretty awesome."

"Oh, she is. You two would get along, I think."

"Oh yeah?"

"Yeah. She, like you, puts at least *some* faith in the whole TV dating scene. She loves that kind of stuff."

Ivy chuckled. "Hmm. I like her already." She lifted a hand to her forehead as she spoke, then lightly traced her fingers over the bandage.

Easton leaned in to inspect the dressing. "Is it bothering you?" He hoped it wasn't getting infected.

"Kind of. It just started throbbing out of nowhere," she said.

"Maybe our conversation was giving you a headache," he joked.

Ivy gave him a playful slap. "It's not. But it *is* tugging at my heartstrings a little."

And *she* was tugging at his. "How about I take a look at that wound?"

At his request, Ivy scooted in closer, reminding him of the way she'd done that very thing the night before. While asking him to kiss her, that is. The mere recollection made his mouth water. It almost made him regret not breaking out the peaches.

Of course, if anything were to happen between them, which was something he was feeling a lot more open to, Easton wouldn't want the moment to be stemmed by an artificial high or a loss of inhibition.

"Let me grab the kit," he said, standing to make his way over to the cabinet. He hurried back to her and, with careful, glove-covered hands, pried the corner of the tape from her hairline. He caught hints of that sweet vanilla scent as he pulled in a shallow breath, inspecting the wound carefully. The gash had clotted nicely, and was already sealing shut. "No sign of infection," he told her. "But the dressing needs to be changed out."

He quickly prepared a few strips of tape, sensing Ivy's gaze on him all the while.

He tried very hard not to get distracted as he cleaned the area, applied ointment, and prepared a new mesh bandage, but he couldn't help but hear her musings from the night before—she'd been wondering what it would be like to kiss him.

Were similar thoughts running through her mind tonight, or had that simply been the moonshine talking?

Ivy had hummed off and on as he attended to her, yet only as Easton applied the final piece of medical tape did he recognize the song.

"You singing Christmas carols for me?" he asked, realizing that she was likely used to hearing carols this time of year. "Are you the type that listens to Christmas music on your own, or just at the mall and parties?"

She seemed to consider that. "I used to listen to it on my own."

"But not anymore?" Easton asked in a whisper. He took longer than necessary to press gently at the corners of the tape, a sudden urge coming over him—the urge to press a kiss to her covered wound. Before he could reconsider, Easton was already leaning closer.

"I've been…busy." Her reply came out even quieter than his.

He cupped the sides of her face, a great sense of tenderness coming over him.

Ivy's eyes drifted shut. Tentatively then, she lifted her hands and wrapped them around his wrists encouragingly, her silky fingers warm against his skin.

Softly then, Easton pressed a gentle kiss over the bandage.

"Merry Christmas, Ivy," he said under his breath. He pulled back the slightest bit as he realized something—a drastic shift in the energy between them.

Gone was the playful tone that dwelled during stories of her past. Gone was the darkness that lingered as he revisited his. Here, in the space surrounding them now, was a pure and powerful chemistry that made his pulse rev, his breath hitch, and his lower belly heat up with anticipation.

Ivy lifted her chin, confirming, with the heavy set of her lids, that she felt it too. She licked her lips, leaving firelight to reflect along the pretty upper peaks and the full curve of her perfect pout.

The physical sensations spiked up a notch as he considered tasting those lips once and for all. Pulse spiking. Heart pounding. Reservations gone. He lowered his head and traced, ever so gently, the shape of her mouth with his bottom lip, testing, savoring. If he was going through with this, allowing himself to give in to the magnetic pull of passion, he wouldn't hold back.

With that, Easton parted his lips ever so slightly and moved in to kiss her at last. He sampled the soft surface of her mouth once, then twice before coming in for a long, lingering kiss. The belly heat roared hotter still as he tilted his head and came in for more of the same. More of her.

A breathy whimper sounded in her throat as Ivy's hand moved up the back of his neck. Her fingers ventured into his hair, causing another thrill to sprout low in his core.

Easton wasn't sure where their rendezvous would lead in the days ahead, but as he enjoyed the silky heat of Ivy's mouth, and the seductive sound of her sigh, he assured himself that he wouldn't take it further than this—her kiss.

That suited him just fine. As long as she'd have him, even if it was the whole night through, Easton would attend to her with his kisses, his touch, and the warmth of his body beside hers. Tomorrow would bring what it may, but for now, he'd enjoy tonight with the fascinating Ivy Ingles in his arms.

CHAPTER 10

If Ivy thought sleeping before a crackling fire was nice, kissing in the warmth of those glowing flames was sheer bliss.

Easton might not believe in love, but that hadn't stopped him from mastering the art of kissing. Mastering it to the point he hadn't pushed for anything more. And why push when their moments of passion were already perfect?

It was as if he knew that the sensation of his lips on hers would offer more romance, wonderment, and delight than she'd known in a very long time.

She'd carried those moments into a sound and satisfied sleep, ever aware that she might very well spend Christmas Day with Easton, right there on a mountain range in snow-covered Colorado.

Even now as she prepared the table for a very non-traditional breakfast on Christmas morning—stale cinnamon rolls, moonshine peaches, and beef jerky—a blend of contentment and peace settled over her.

She glanced at the door, wondering how much longer Easton would be gone. Earlier that morning, he'd laced a pair of snowshoes and headed for the lodge with his cell phone. Once he was able to get service, he planned to text his sister with an update and check on the latest weather forecast. If the whistling wind pushing against the structure was any indication, the blizzard wasn't done with them yet.

When she'd first arrived at the yurt two days ago, Ivy wanted nothing more than to catch the next flight out. But now, as she waited for the heroic Easton to burst back through that door with news of the storm and road conditions, she secretly hoped they'd be snowed in for another day.

Just admitting the fact caused a spurt of fear to shoot through her. Things between them had been going so well, a part of her feared she'd only spoil it. It was that insecure side of her piping up again. The side that said she wasn't fascinating enough to keep a man interested long-term. The side that said it'd be best to end things while she was ahead. At least then she could enjoy the moments they'd shared. If she stayed and things ended in some form of rejection, those memories might be ruined.

At that thought, the door flung open. That wind she'd been hearing roared full force.

Ivy glanced up, expecting to see Easton's massive form filling the doorway. He was there all right, but he was dragging something close to his own size along with him. Something with a powder covered trunk and frost-covered branches.

No way. He'd gotten a tree? The sentiment caused a pool of tingly heat to ripple through her body. She hurried over and pushed the door closed behind him with a grunt, then twisted the knob as he'd instructed to lock it in place.

Already, the delectably spicy scent of pine filled the space, making it feel exactly like Christmas Day.

"Ho, ho, ho," Easton cheered, giving the tree a quick shake. Snow fell from the branches, turning the pine needles from frosted white to a rich, forest green.

"This is beautiful," she said, watching as he hoisted the tree enough to lower the trunk into a small log structure on the floor. He must have fashioned it before leaving, she realized.

"Well," he said. "I figured, if the roads and airports were still closed, I'd saw down a tree on my way back."

Ivy loved the way he'd said it. As if sawing down a pine tree and dragging it through a blizzard was no big deal. She also liked that, to Easton, it really wasn't. The buff and manly traits in him made Easton all the more attractive. But something new was taking precedence in her mind—the roads and airports were still closed.

"So we'll be here another night probably?" she confirmed.

Easton gave her a nod. "Definitely through the night. But they think there's going to be a nice break in the storm tomorrow. Enough that they can get the canyon roads open again, and probably the flights moving as well." He stepped away from the tree once it was balanced within the makeshift stand and moved to her side with his chest puffed. "Well, what do you think?"

The gorgeous tree with its heavenly scent made her smile. Her heart warmed and swelled with gratitude. "I *really* love it," she breathed. "Thank you."

"You're welcome." He tugged a backpack from his shoulder and unzipped the side. "I stopped by one of the other yurts on my way back and grabbed this, in case you wanted to decorate it somehow." He tugged a rather large Ziplock bag from his bag and handed it to her.

Ivy inspected the pack through the clear bag, realizing it held an array of craft supplies. Balls of colorful yarn were shoved at the base of the bag, while popsicle sticks, scissors, and glue sat on top.

The inspiration and childlike joy that came over her made her smile grow even more. "We can definitely make some cool decorations from this."

"I figured as much." Easton returned her smile with a gorgeous grin of his own, then tipped his head to shake the snow from his hair with his fingers.

"You might want to turn your back for a minute so I can change," he said, moving quickly to where his clothes from the day before hung dry. At once he was unfastening his jeans.

"Oh," Ivy blurted, turning so that her back faced him. She traced a finger along the edge of the bag while she waited for him to get changed. She could hardly believe this was the same guy who'd made the snide remarks about her having an *in* with Mother Earth. And the same guy who'd actually said, back on the phone when she'd called to confirm, he'd find a way to keep her warm at night on the chance they got snowed in.

Ivy hadn't thought for a second that would ever happen, yet here they were. Another one of his comments came to mind, this one from the interview. "So," she started, a wry chuckle forming at her lips. "For Christmas dinner, are we going to cook up your latest kill?" she asked.

"Heh, if only it were that easy to hunt in a blizzard. The wildlife has ducked for cover. But I *did* get a little something special from the other yurt. You can turn around now, by the way," he said, coming up behind her and securing the backpack once more. He pulled two cans from the bag, cans she recognized as clam chowder. He removed a third that Ivy couldn't identify without leaning closer.

"Are those peaches?"

"Moonshine-*free* peaches," he stipulated. "Can't have Ivy The Lightweight taking down any more of those spiked ones, can we?"

"I guess it's best if I avoid them," she admitted.

"At least until *tonight*," Easton added. The insinuative tone coating those words caused an untamed thrill to shoot through her chest.

Ivy chuckled, but inwardly, she was thinking back on something else Easton had said about the storm. It would likely break tomorrow, allowing him to go to his place and Ivy to hers.

A sense of sadness threatened to take over at the thought, but she forced herself to focus elsewhere. Ivy had a choice to make, after all. Last night, she and Easton had shared some incredible moments. Deep conversation, passionate kisses, and a whole lot of laughs too.

Now, knowing they'd likely part ways tomorrow, Ivy could give in to another day and night of the same—if that's what he wanted too—or she could rely on her no-dating directive and put things to a halt. The first option, as wonderful as it might be, would leave her vulnerable at the end. Her heart nearly stung at the thought. The second option, like the rule itself, would shield her heart from hurt and her head from worry.

She joined Easton at the table while testing both options in her mind, wondering if he was inwardly doing the same. If he *was* open to a second night of curling up with her beside the fire, would Ivy really have it in her to reject him and deny herself?

She'd know soon enough where Easton stood, which meant Ivy needed to decide for herself as well.

Already, as she watched the polite way he slid his canteen her way, nodding that she should take a drink, Ivy knew what her choice would be. Men like Easton were few and far between. It might be easy to activate her rule if the attraction were nothing more than physical. But things with Easton went much deeper, and as vulnerable as it might make her—opening her heart to him—Ivy couldn't really imagine it any other way. If there was a chance this could actually somehow work out between them, she would take it.

She ignored the spot of fear that cut its way in at the thought, and focused on the moment instead. They had today—Christmas Day, in fact—and Ivy planned to make the most of it.

Easton looked over the impressive array of handmade ornaments along the table. Yarn, twigs, and popsicle sticks—that's really all it had taken. In the firelight's glow, he watched Ivy fasten the final cross from two twigs, a loving expression on her face as she wrapped brown yarn around the cross-points.

She reached for a strand of red next and proceeded to fasten a loop for hanging before tying a small bow in the front.

"There," she said, a satisfied grin on her face. "We've got a dozen of each now. You ready to decorate?"

"Almost," he said. "I've got a little something to make the decorating part a little more…festive." Easton moved over to his backpack. There, his phone was connected to his wireless charging box. He'd known he'd need to be selective with the power source, considering the duration of their stay was undetermined, but he'd done more than just check the weather and get a tree on his trip out. He'd downloaded a list of Christmas tunes onto his phone as well. Ones that might help Ivy, away from her family as she was, enjoy some of the Christmas spirit she talked about. He'd done something extra as well, but Easton planned to save that surprise for later.

"Here," he said, propping the phone on the table and pressing play on the playlist he'd made. He started with "Oh Holy Night" and turned up the sound. "Now I'm ready."

Ivy stared at the phone in wonder, then turned her wide eyes on him. "You've got Christmas music on your phone?"

He shrugged, noting the moisture that welled in her eyes. "I was able to download a few songs while checking the weather."

Gratitude. That's what he saw on her face as she shook her head and sniffed. "That was thoughtful, Easton. Come here," she demanded, wiping at her eyes with the back of her hands. She held her arms out to him as he neared her, making her intent clear—she meant to hug him for the efforts he'd put in. That was fine by him.

He stepped into the blessed space between her extended arms, happy to wrap his around her as well.

Ivy curled into his embrace. "Thank you," she breathed against his shoulder.

It felt nice there, very nice. Ivy's heated body, silky and soft against his. He closed his eyes and let himself take in the moment.

The soft, beautiful melody lulled them into a longer exchange, their bodies melding together. Ivy pressed her cheek against his chest and inhaled a deep, calming breath, but she didn't drop her arms just yet. Instead, she began to caress his shoulders, softly, gently, as she held him in place.

A rush of goosebumps surfaced over his skin as she repeated the action. Easton rested his hands at her hips and swayed with her. "Dance with me?" he asked.

She grinned up at him, and rested a hand in his. "I'd love to."

Easton wrapped a hand around hers, noting the delicate feel of it compared to his. She was so soft and silky and warm. She was sensitive, kind, and rather cheery considering the circumstance. He'd enjoyed the way she taught him to make the simple ornaments, with such a plain and childlike joy. He imagined sitting around a dinner table with little ones and felt the first longings of fatherly desire he'd ever known.

If they could have a mother like her...perhaps they'd be happy and well. Assuming they had a father like *him*, an inner voice specified. A voice that surprised him. It wasn't that Easton hadn't known he was good with the teens he worked with. His past experiences gave him an edge when helping the troubled youth who came through the center. But to see himself as a father? That idea was foreign to him. Until his time with Ivy Ingles put new ideas into his head.

Even as he held her then, her small form warm against him,

he had different urges. The desire to love and care for a woman in ways he never thought he'd know. He wanted to keep her safe too. Perhaps the protective inclinations stemmed from his initial rescue efforts as he searched for her in the storm, perhaps they stemmed from something more, he wasn't really sure. One thing he *was* certain of was that he was pleased they had more time together.

As the music rang out, the flames doing a dance of their own, Easton flattened his hand along Ivy's back, willing her to feel what he was feeling. The heat, the connection, the...the *joy* the song filled in for him.

Yes, that seemed fitting. He did feel joy, and peace too. It was different from the kind of solitude he sought when stepping onto the open land, ready to be at one with nature and his surroundings. Because feeling, in a way, at one with *her*... nothing compared to it.

When Easton sensed the song was coming to an end, he moved a hand slowly down the length of her back, enjoying the way she curled into him beneath his chin as they rocked gently back and forth. Back and forth. Loving the warmth of her in his arms. The feel of her against his palm.

Gently then, he moved his hand smoothly up the length of her back, lightly massaging her along the way, and rounded her shoulder next. Softly, he traced his fingers over the covered and bare parts alike, backing away just enough to cup her elbows. He couldn't help but set his eyes on her, testing the thoughts in his mind. The energy in the charged space. Was what he was feeling real? Was she feeling it too?

She glanced up at him shyly, blinking twice before curling into him once more. And then her hands were moving up and over his shoulders, caressing his neck, the broad span of his back, pulling him closer as a sigh passed through her lips. "I'm glad we got stuck in the storm," she admitted, so softly he almost missed it.

Every part of him seemed to register that tidbit in some way. His pulse rushed, his lower belly went fire hot, and his mind scattered like ashes in a windstorm. He cradled her closer and smiled. "Me too, Ivy."

The next song came in with a bit of a ruckus. "Jingle Bells." The cheery sound and familiar beat took them from the quiet, rather intimate moment to a more playful feel. He cupped her hand and moved into a jive dance with her.

"Did you know Jingle Bells was originally meant to be a Thanksgiving song?" he asked, giving her a twirl.

"No." She giggled as he pulled her into him once more. She moved her feet to keep up while wrapping her hand around his back.

"Apparently, the composer had it played on Thanksgiving Day in Sunday school. It was supposed to commemorate the Medford sleigh races."

"I didn't know that," Ivy said. "Did *you* know that it was also the first song broadcast from space?" she offered.

Dang, he liked this. Liked having somebody one step ahead of him. "No," he lied. "I didn't know that." A rush of anticipation stirred within him as Easton contemplated the hours ahead. Sure, Ivy might have been a mere stranger to him just days ago, but somehow, being stuck in a yurt with her seemed like the best thing ever. And, he mused, the perfect way to spend Christmas Day.

CHAPTER 11

Ivy lay on her belly before the fire, Easton at her side. "Okay," he said, "you ready for the next one?"

She'd been propped up on her elbows, but at his prompt, Ivy flattened herself and rested her cheek on the floor. "Ready."

Easton propped a finger at the upper right side of her back, looped it up and around, then came down in a long, straight line. *Easy*. "A candy cane."

"Nope," he said. "A shepherd's hook."

Ivy reached out to give him a playful swat on the leg. "Same thing." She rolled onto her back then and propped the back of her head with her hands to look up at him. Easton's expression shifted as she held his gaze, his smile replaced with...well, she dared say adoration.

"I could stay here with you for another week," he said. The comment ignited a delicious fire within her, the heat sizzling all the way down her back. "I almost wish we *would* be stuck here a little longer."

Her heart clanked out a few extra beats.

"I'm sure you're anxious to get back to your family though," he was quick to add. His brow furrowed as he turned his gaze toward the fire and draped his arms across his bent knees. "I bet Chantelle's getting impatient too," he mumbled.

Ivy studied him as he narrowed his gaze at the flames. She got the sense he regretted saying what he had, about wishing they could stay longer. She hadn't forgotten what he'd told her the other night—that he didn't believe in love. And as guarded as she'd been over the years, Ivy knew Easton's reservations went much deeper. So what would happen after today? He'd just go back to his life of solitude? Sure, he had coworkers and clients coming through, but would he ever really give his heart to someone?

And what if her wishful thinking stemmed from a place that wondered the same thing? A place that said if he and Ivy had enough time together, he might just overcome his objections completely?

The thought planted an ache deep in her chest. Part of her wanted to assure him that she felt the same. She'd love to spend another week with him there. But another part of her, the part that said it was best to quit while she was ahead, was glad their time would end before he could discover the parts that made her...easy to leave. Better to end things on a good note, remain mysterious, and know that he left liking her the way she liked him.

But what if that thought was selfish? It was cowardly, in the least of it. Because wasn't Easton worth the risk? If he truly *was* finding a unique connection with her, if there really was potential for something more, one of them would have to push past their fears and do something about it.

*I could stay here with you another week...*His comment came to her mind, suggesting that, in a way, Easton *had* put himself out there.

Come on, Ivy. Tell him you're not in a hurry to get back. That you're barely missing your family because he's made the day so special and fun. And romantic...

"I almost forgot," Easton said, hurrying to a stand and heading toward the cupboard.

A blend of relief and disappointment sunk through her. Gone was the pressure of stepping out of her comfort zone. But also gone was her chance to assure Easton that she felt the same.

"I got you one last surprise while I was out," he said. "After we sent your family that text, we weren't able to stick around where the internet connection was to get their response. So today, I took your phone with me, turned it on while I was in range, and let it receive all your texts."

A rush of excitement shot through her at the idea of hearing from her family. "You did?" She was quick to sit up as he joined her back at the fireplace, phone in hand.

"I did," he assured. "I also sent them another text that said we're still safe and still waiting for the storm to clear."

Now it was gratitude rushing in. "That was so thoughtful," she said as she took the phone from him. "Thank you."

Her family hadn't disappointed. There were over eighty missed texts on her family group chat. She hovered her thumb over the screen as a grin pulled at her lips. "You ready?"

Easton's brows lifted. "You're going to share with me?" he asked, already scooting in closer.

"Of course." The warmth from his closeness felt like a promise. There *had* to be more to this. So much more. But then she noticed something. Her battery was higher than it'd been before. "This was at twelve percent earlier," she said, baffled.

"I have a battery pack, so I gave it a little juice to keep it going."

"Ah," she tipped her head back. Of course.

The text thread opened up with dozens of bubbles filled with holiday greetings, photos from the Christmas Eve party, and...*assumptions* about what Ivy was up to?

In her effort to breeze past the long thread and up to the top, Ivy had spotted a text from her teasing brother, Ronny: *Hope Ivy's cuddling up to the Colorado bachelor to stay warm tonight. Kissy, kissy....* Kissing emojis followed.

"Looks like they're talking about me too," Easton pointed out.

Ivy's face flushed with heat. She glanced up at him, wondering if perhaps she'd made a mistake by not looking over the messages by herself first. It'd be impossible to filter through them with Easton so close.

A wide grin spread over his handsome face as she contemplated. "C'mon, Ivy. Don't back out now." He followed up with a playful nudge to her shoulder, his against hers.

Her heart skipped a beat, maybe more, as she grinned back at him. *Worth it.* This was worth whatever humiliation they dished. She didn't want Easton to move even an inch away from her.

She glanced back down to see she'd made it all the way to

the top of the thread, where she'd sent her text about the storm. "Okay," she said. "Here goes nothing."

Mom was first to start off the comments, expressing relief for the fact that she was okay. The motion was seconded by the others until her sister piped up about something that caused another streak of embarrassment to push through her.

Jackie: *Samuel Leemon is going to have his heart broken! He came into town yesterday and asked Mom if he could join us.*

"Who's Samuel?" Easton asked.

"Just an old neighbor kid," she said, feeling the heat flare up in her face once more. She hadn't thought about Samuel in years.

"Poor guy," Easton said. "He came home for the holidays to finally score the girl next door, and she's off getting seduced by some bachelor gone rogue."

Now it felt like her face might explode. "He didn't come back for me."

"The hell he didn't..." He mumbled it so softly Ivy wasn't sure she'd heard him correctly. "Tell me this," he challenged. "Did you two ever kiss?"

Ivy shook her head, a smile pulling at her lips. "Barely," she admitted. "We were little."

"And he's never stopped thinking about you," Easton said in a dramatic, TV host type of voice. He lifted a hand and spanned it before him. "He's gone out, made a name for himself, all so he could impress Ivy Ingles from Tanglewood Lane. And *you* weren't even there."

"That's enough." She giggled some more, nudging him in return before setting her gaze back on the screen. "Oh, look, pictures!" Thank heavens. This whole topic of Samuel was making her blush. Although, she'd be lying if she said she didn't enjoy the jealous tone of his response.

"That's everyone," she said, pausing for him to take in the group.

Easton leaned in and squinted, a pleased expression on his face. "This is the whole group? Everyone but you?"

"Everyone but me." Ivy pointed out who was who, all the way down to her nephews, nieces, and their grumpy cat, Doug.

"What kind of name is Doug for a cat?" Easton asked.

But Ivy only shook her head. "I liked a guy named Doug at the time."

"People really do that?" He scrunched his face.

"Twelve-year-old girls do. At least, this one did."

Enlightenment crossed his features. "*That* explains it."

"Explains what?"

He shrugged dismissively. "Oh, all the girls at *my* middle school had pets named Easton. Cats, dogs, birds, goldfish..."

Ivy chuckled. "I bet they did." Boy, was that the truth. No doubt Easton had been breaking hearts since he could flash that grin of his.

She quickly skimmed past the part where Ronny bugged her about the bachelor she'd be snuggling up to all night to stay warm. Ivy was certain she'd gotten away with it until he spoke up.

"Wait, wait, I think you missed a few."

"I'll read them later," she assured.

"Aw, you're no fun. Let me see it." Easton held out his hand expectantly.

Ivy nearly gasped at his boldness and tucked it behind her back. "Like I would ever hand this to you."

"You might if I do this." He gave her waist a testing poke with his finger.

A squeal snuck out of her lips as she twisted away.

"Ooh, what do we have here?" Easton gave the other side of her waist a playful squeeze, earning a giggle and another squeal.

Ivy released the phone behind her back and reached for his hands, trying to stop them from tickling her any further.

A small wrestle ensued—Ivy squirming beyond his grasp while Easton made up the distance, and soon he was hovered over her, the two in a whirl of laughter and jagged breaths.

"I *love* that you're ticklish," Easton said, buffering her from his full weight as he inspected her in the fire's glow. Her arms were pinned at her sides now, which was a problem, since a stray lock of hair rested on her cheek. Ivy attempted to blow if off.

"You're going to have to release my hands," she said breathlessly, "or get my hair out of my face for me."

Easton held her gaze inquisitively. "If *I* get the stray strand, I'll have to release *your* hands and I'm not willing to do that just yet."

Ivy shook her head as the piece started to itch her face. "Hurry, hurry, it feels *awful*!"

"Alright then." He lowered his head then, bringing his face to hers. Her heart sputtered out of beat. She was just about to ask him what he was doing when she felt his lips part slightly at her cheek. He pinned the strand between his lips, then lifted himself away from her and released it with a small push of air.

"There you go, princess. Shall I feed you grapes next? Fan your face while you recline before the fire?"

She grinned, loving this playful side of him. The side that

made her feel as if he was hers and she was his and that nothing could possibly separate them. A recollection came to her then, of the moment she'd wanted to speak up earlier.

"Easton?" she said, daring herself to be brave. To chance ruining everything. "I..."

He lifted a brow. The expression made him look just like a dashing actor on the big screen. "Yes?"

Anxiety shot through her in the quiet pause. Maybe telling him wasn't the best way. Perhaps showing him would be better. "I don't want any grapes," she said. "Or the fan. But there *is* something I *would* like." Arms still pinned to her sides, she moved her gaze, very pointedly, to his mouth.

Ivy could hardly believe she'd said what she had. It sounded more forward than she'd imagined, and it too, had taken a level of bravery to voice. But as Easton narrowed his eyes and fixed his gaze on her mouth in return, she knew she'd said the perfect thing.

He lowered his head to hers and paused once their lips were all but touching. Ivy released a shallow breath, wondering if he'd wait like he had before, perhaps start off with another round of testing kisses. But he moved right in instead, pressing a long, fervent kiss to her lips. She'd asked him to kiss her, after all, and it seemed he planned to deliver with a flourish.

She reveled in the warm, measured weight of him as he kissed her again. And then again. The short facial hair around his lips only added to the sensation, giving life to Easton's rugged appeal. His scruff might be rough like sandpaper, but his lips were smooth, soft, and oh so pleasing.

With his hands at her wrists, Easton lifted her arms at either side, then slipped his fingers through hers and kissed her again. And again.

So good.

He moved his attentions along her jawline next, pressing hot kisses in a trail to her earlobe, then down her neck, where he circled the hollow of her throat.

"Mmm..." he rasped, the deep sound causing a thrill of its own.

With what felt like slow deliberation, Easton unlocked his fingers from hers and traced his hands, ever so gently, down her inner arms, leaving a trail of delicious heat in his wake.

Goosebumps rippled over her skin.

His touch drifted off as he rounded the bend in her arms, then picked back up as he cupped her hips, his warm grip urging her closer still.

Ivy used her free hands to explore the hair at the back of his head, gripping at the bearskin rug with the other. She'd never felt such bliss, and it seemed her body could hardly contain it.

Her breath turned jagged as the heat of his mouth trailed back up to her earlobe. He surprised her by taking a teasing taste, his teeth slightly scraping her skin, seeming to know it would send another thrill to rush through her.

"I don't want you to worry," he said under his breath, kissing the side of her neck, then teasing her skin with his short, scratchy scruff. "We don't have to do more than this."

He kissed her again while her mind reeled. In one sense Ivy was relieved that he wouldn't press for more; she'd had some very uncomfortable moments with pushy men in her past. But she couldn't help but wonder what urged him to make it known. He was a gentleman, that much was evident in his conduct, which could answer her question in and of itself. But perhaps he was already very certain that he didn't want anything with her beyond their time in the yurt. If that was the case, he'd certainly not want to use her in such a way.

Stop, Ivy. Just enjoy this time. Wherever it *might lead.*

She pulled back slightly, inspecting Easton in the low light as an ache settled into her heart. She wanted to say something. Anything. *I'm really falling for you, Easton. Do you think there's a chance for this to work out? Could you maybe somehow believe in love?*

The furrow in Easton's brow, the intensity behind his eyes, said he was stuck in his head as well.

Her heart seemed to slow as she sensed he might pull away and put an end to their night completely.

No, Easton. Let's not end it yet.

He blinked, ran a thumb over her lower lip, and looked into her eyes once again. "Ivy," he said, and then moved in to kiss her once more. This time there was a certainty behind the strong lock of his lips on hers. In the way he tilted his head and deepened the kiss, showing confidence. Conviction. And sureness about what he wanted. And skill too. Always such mastered movements that, even now, pulled a whimper from her throat as she kissed him in return. *So good.*

Whether he was set on convincing her or convincing himself, Ivy sensed that Easton wanted to push past his struggle with love. The question was, would he really be able to do it, or was Ivy destined to suffer a broken heart?

CHAPTER 12

A series of loud and angry sounding thumps yanked Easton from sleep. His eyes shot open as he pushed himself off the floor. Instinctively, he darted a look toward the fireplace to ensure Ivy was safe. Once he caught a glimpse of her tucked into the sleeping bag, he turned to the door.

Another series of thumps came—knocks, he realized as he jumped to his feet. Ivy stirred in her sleeping bag. "What *is* tha—" But then she gasped mid-word. "A *bear?*"

"Take it easy, Goldilocks," Easton said. "I don't think bears knock." He leaned toward the door, guessing at who it might be. "Hello?"

"Officer Freeman here with highway patrol," came a voice.

He'd guessed right, which meant the canyon roads were officially clear. He glanced over his shoulder. "You decent?" he asked. "Want me to give you a moment to put your clothes back on, Goldie?"

She laughed. "Stop it. I'm dressed, of course."

He chuckled too and twisted the knob. Cold air wafted into the yurt as he tugged the door open—a drastic change to the blustery blizzard. "How can we help you, officer?"

"I saw your Jeep up there, and the smoke from your structure here, and hoped you might be able to explain the SUV we found off the roadside midway through the canyon."

"Oh, yes, sir. That belongs to my...friend. She's right over there. In her very own sleeping bag," he added.

"Hi there." Ivy waved and came to a stand. "I got stuck on my way up the day before Christmas Eve, and Easton was good enough to come get me."

The officer's eyes went wide in question. "You two got snowed in up here, eh?"

"We did," Easton said. "But I'm guessing the roads are open now?"

"We put our best plows to work, threw some salt and sand down too. The entire pass is good to go."

Disappointment struck him at the confirmation. "That's great news, officer."

The man nodded, looking from Easton to Ivy, then back again. "Well, it'd be best if you could clear the stranded vehicle from the roadside within the next few hours or so."

"Oh, we will," Easton assured. He shouldn't harbor any ill will toward the man for doing his job, but he couldn't help but be irritated by the way he'd pressed about the SUV.

"Very well." The man looked down at his snow-covered boots. "You don't happen to have a pair of snowshoes I could borrow for the trip back, do you? I could lean them up against the lodge when I'm through..."

"Sure," Easton said, lifting a pair off the hook and handing them over. "Here you go." Under different circumstances, Easton might invite the man inside to strap them onto his boots. As it was, he didn't feel like inviting the party crasher himself to barge in for the party's final moments. "You have a good day."

"You do the same," he said with a nod. "And be safe out there."

Easton returned the man's nod before closing the door. It took him a moment to spin around and see, for the last time, the gorgeous sight of Ivy standing in the firelight. He spun slowly, his mind drifting back to the passionate moments they'd shared the night before. He hadn't wanted to stop kissing her. And if Easton hadn't started to worry that his self-control might slip as the night went on, he might very well *still* be kissing those tempting lips of hers. Until the officer had come by, anyway.

"I can't believe they got it all cleared up out there." Disbelief coated her words. He detected a somber tone as well, as if she were no happier about the news than he was.

He thought back to his musings from the night before. An idea had come to mind. One that said he could just…*try* having a relationship with Ivy and see where it went, if she was up for it. Sure, the distance might be enough to keep things from really going anywhere, but it had to be worth a try.

Easton could barely even believe his own mindset. It was as if someone else had climbed into his head and shoveled out the layers of pessimism and doubt. Not all of them, but enough that he was tempted to speak up and see if she felt the same.

"I feel really bad that you did so many nice things for me, even giving me gifts with the tree, the Christmas carols, and the texts you downloaded for me…" She lowered her gaze to the sleeping bag she'd rolled up. "I'm thinking of something I might be able to gift in return, but—"

"I appreciate that," Easton interrupted," but I doubt we have time for…*that*." He lifted an insinuative brow. "Plus, you just rolled the sleeping bag up."

Ivy tossed a pillow in his direction and smacked him upside the head. "You're terrible."

Easton grinned as a vision ran through his mind. A playful pillow fight with Ivy, wrestling and laughing while tiny feathers got caught in her hair. Another very dreary wave of gloom sank in. Saying goodbye to Ivy was going to suck.

"What I had in mind," she said, tucking the sleeping bag back into the cupboard, "was maybe deleting the interview. I'm not sure what I would tell Marsha since she's got her heart set on you being on the show, I know it…"

Wait, she might actually be able to get him out of the show? Not that he was certain to be picked like Ivy thought he was, but still.

Ivy busied herself by tidying up as she continued. "I might be able to say that, I don't know, something went wrong with the recording. Or that my battery ran out a few minutes into it and I didn't even notice." She and Nancy never touched one another's work, after all. And it wasn't as if she'd labeled the file. It was just sitting there, a blank folder with the date. One Ivy could delete once she got the chance.

"I wouldn't want you to take any heat at your job over it," he said, coming up alongside her where she tucked the pillows into the cupboard as well. "Here," he said softly, reaching for the laundry bag in one of the cubbies. He proceeded to tug the pillows from their place and remove the cases. "We can take these up to the lodge on our way out. The kids, depending on where they're at in the program, don't often get those sorts of luxuries. These accommodations are more for the staff. "

"I hate lying," Ivy blurted, proving her thoughts were still on the dilemma, "but I don't think you should have to go onto that show if you don't want to."

Easton snatched the hand towel off the table, tucked it into the laundry tote, and walked over to drop it beside the door. It was obvious there was more at work in that mind of hers, as there was in his too. They'd just had a couple of amazing days together and now it was all going to come to an end.

"I don't want me to have to do the show either," he said. "Maybe if you hand me your phone and let *me* do the deleting, you'll be off the hook and we all win. We'd have to get rid of the contract too, right?"

Ivy's shoulders dropped. Her face fell flat, and the look in her eyes seemed to be a million miles away. Because they weren't *really* talking about the recording and the contract and the idea of him doing the show. Or at least, that's not what *he* was thinking about.

Easton watched as Ivy shuffled over to the fire and plopped down on the rug. The flames had gotten pretty low, and Easton wasn't sure if he should build it back up or let it die out completely.

A pain ripped through him as he realized that the alternatives applied to his and Ivy's relationship too. As new and uncertain as it was, things could develop and build into something amazing or they could fizzle out altogether. So which would it be? And was he the one who was supposed to bring it up? The massive moose in the room? The question neither of them had an answer for…

Ivy reached out and patted the spot beside her. "Come here," she prompted.

Yes, it was definitely on her mind too.

One step in her direction, that's all it took for his fear to descend. *Just tell her that you're too broken to love someone in that way.* But Easton knew that was a lie. Loving someone hadn't been the issue. Trusting that love could lead to a happy, fulfilled life—that was the real trick.

He shuffled toward her in slow steps, hoping to somehow get his mind in order before he joined her. Once he was at her side on the rug, Easton lowered himself beside Ivy and stared at the fire as well. "Hi."

"Hi."

"Did you know that in a wildfire, water deep inside a tree can turn to steam and make the tree explode?" he asked.

Ivy shook her head, then leaned over and plopped it dramatically against his arm. She groaned. "I'm really going to miss you, Easton."

Her confession fanned at the ache in his chest. He wrapped an arm around her back and pulled her into his side. "I'm going to miss you too, Ivy."

"I know I should be glad that we can get back to life as usual, but…" Her words died off there, but Easton knew just what she meant.

He cleared his throat and responded to the urging voice in his head. "Maybe we can just—" It sounded like that last word had been chopped off with an axe. In a sense, it had; fear was very much like a razor-sharp blade, a force capable of severing one from life's fulfillment and promise.

"Just *what?*" Ivy prompted.

He turned toward her then, not sure he'd be able to mean what he wanted to say. Her blue eyes, so prodding and unsure, seemed to plead with him. "I know you said you don't believe in love," she started.

"I'd like to give it a try," he said softly. "I'm not sure what that would look like with you in LA and me out here, but I want to keep talking to you. Catching up with you after a long day at work. See how things go." Sure, it was a rather anticlimactic declaration, but it was the most he could muster.

"I'd like that too," she said, concern slipping away from her features. She smiled, sighed loudly, then brought her cheek to rest against his bicep.

There. He'd done it. He hadn't made any promises, but he hadn't broken things off either. He'd left an open door which was, for Easton, an accomplishment in itself. Perhaps once he told his sister about all of this, she'd forgive him for not going on the show. The idea caught fire in his mind. That was it. He'd just tell Chantelle that he *asked* Ivy to delete the footage because he was interested in *her,* which was true. And besides, his sister's goal was to help Easton open up to the idea of love. Something he was at least trying to do.

"Tell your boss I changed my mind about the show, will you? That will take the heat off of you."

Ivy pulled back to glance up at him. "But then you'll take heat from your sister if she finds out."

"I'll tell her myself," he said. "She'll understand." Now it was Easton's turn to let out a relieved sigh as the tension drained from his body. More tightness and ache than he'd even been aware of.

Within the next hour or so, he and Ivy would pack up, head out, and say their goodbyes. But for now, he'd enjoy spending a little more time with her, soft and warm by his side.

CHAPTER 13

"Thanks for following me back to the airport," Ivy said after returning the SUV. Turned out the extra insurance had come in handy. The rock had put a hefty dent in the front bumper, but that was nothing compared to what could have happened had she *not* hit the rock. *Thank the Lord.*

She shivered, more from the thought than the weather. The sun was out today, shining on them as they walked along the outdoor walkway, which made her thin coat finally adequate for the weather. Still, as warm as the rays of sunshine felt against her skin, Easton was even warmer.

"I was happy to do it. Besides, I couldn't have you get stuck someplace on your way back. Who knows if the car rental guy would try to swoop to your rescue and take you back to his secret dwelling in the woods."

She laughed, but the sight of the double doors brought her mind back to the task at hand. Saying goodbye to Easton. She slowed, and he did the same, bringing her rolling luggage to a halt. She turned to face him, resting her hands on his chest, and reminded herself that he'd agreed to give this a try. For all the reservations Ivy had regarding love, she inwardly knew Easton's demons reached deeper than her own. Which made his wishes to continue this, to explore where it might lead, a great triumph in her mind.

"This isn't really goodbye," she said. "It's..."

"I'll see you later," he filled in for her.

"Exactly." She nodded and pinned her lips closed.

"Well then, Ivy," Easton said, sliding his hands onto her hips and bringing his mouth very close to her ear. "I'll see you later." He pressed a kiss to her cheek, then pulled back to give her wink.

Her head went light. "See ya," she said, nodding toward the luggage. "I can take that now. The drop-off is right through these doors."

"Okay then." Easton helped her take ahold of her luggage, then gave her hand a final squeeze. "Travel safe."

She nodded. "I will." And then she was off. Hurrying through the door he held open for her and into the crowd. The recollection of his lips at her cheek still sending delicious waves of bliss over her skin. She was probably smiling like a fool. A big goofy love grin that one might spot a mile away.

"How are you doing today, ma'am?" the gentleman across the ticket counter asked.

"Good, thank you." How soon was too soon to text Easton? She wondered what it would be like to go on a trip with him. To hold his hand all the way through the security line. They'd spit fun facts about first flights and outdated laws, and during the flight, Easton would draw pictures on her back and she'd try and guess what they were.

Similar thoughts went through her mind as she made her way toward her gate, waited among a crowd of fellow passengers, and eventually boarded the plane herself. She'd been tempted, at least two dozen times within that forty minute time frame, to send a snarky or flirty text to Easton, but she resisted the urge. Who knew how much would be too much? Or what time frame would feel like too soon?

The thoughts planted her first bout of insecurity over their plan to…to see where things went. Which, when she considered it, wasn't much of a plan after all. Would she be forced to tiptoe around her urges to send him a silly message? Or call about her day? Would his idea of staying in touch look more like a quarterly report with the boss?

The overhead announcements started up, reminding Ivy that it was time to switch her phone to airplane mode. She resigned herself, while digging into her handbag for the device, to the fact that she might not hear from Easton for days. Even if she *did* touch in after landing in LA safe and sound. Yet just as she pulled the phone from her bag, it let out a small buzz in her hand.

A quick glance caused Ivy's heart to take flight.

Easton: Do you know why airplanes have round windows instead of square?

She hurried back with her reply, smiling as she typed it out.

Ivy: No, why?

Easton: Sharp corners from the square windows were compromising the safety of the aircraft. Rounded windows take the pressure better.

Ivy: Nice! I can't wait to make eyes roll when I tell my family that one.

Easton: Already feeling a little lonely. I used to like being alone. Thanks a lot for ruining that.

Ivy grinned. Turned out sarcasm was one of her love languages. She texted out one last reply, knowing she'd have to switch it to airplane mode soon.

Ivy: You're quite welcome. Thanks for making the whole snowed-in thing...

Ivy glanced about the plane, feeling as if she had an audience to witness what she was about to text. Making it what?

Amazing. No, she backspaced and stared at the cursor.

Another announcement sounded overhead.

Wonderful. Romantic. The best time ever...

"Ugh." She tapped the backspace key again. *Thanks for making the whole snowed-in thing...not so bad. I'll be waving from my round window in five.*

Dec 27

Easton: There's something wrong with me.

Ivy: Oh, no! What is it?

Easton: I got poison ivy.

Ivy: Not funny. You know I've heard that one a million times, right?

Easton: Mine's different.

Ivy: Taking the bait. How?

Easton: Mine only goes away when I'm with you. Think we could get snowed in someplace for New Years?

Ivy: If only. Name the place, and I'll be there. By the way. I told Marsha that you backed out. She wasn't happy. In fact, I think she cried a little, but at least you're off the hook.

Easton: I should feel guilty for making you lie, but I'm far too relieved. Thank you for doing that.

Ivy: It was as much for me as it was for you. Turns out I've got a jealous streak. Who knew?

Easton: Is it wrong that I like hearing that?

Ivy: Possibly. But I like that you like it, so I guess we're even.

Dec 28

Ivy: I just realized something.

Easton: What? That you're madly in love with me?

Ivy: That during our two-hour conversation last night, you still never named the place for our snowed-in-over-New-Year's adventure.

Easton: Crap.

Ivy: How are we supposed to get snowed in together if you don't specify where it can happen?

Dec 29

. . .

Easton: The biggest New Year's storm I see coming is in Minnesota. Not sure I could fashion a yurt there during a blizzard, but I could build us a nice snow cave.

Ivy: Of course you could. My very own caveman, that's what you are. But I have one crucial question.

Easton: Hit me with it.

Ivy: Will there be moonshine peaches?

Easton: Definitely

Dec 31

Ivy: Happy New Year. I forgot to tell you last night—I shared the square window fact with my family—they were riveted. Any fun plans for this evening?

*Easton: What do you mean? I'm waiting for you in a brightly marked snow cave in Minnesota like we planned. Is this a prank? You're waiting outside my snow cave right now, aren't you? *Checking...*

Ivy: Yep, you caught me. I'm here. Trying to wave, but my extremities won't move. I'm using voice-to-text until my lips freeze shut.

Easton: I'm very good at thawing frozen lips. As long as they're your *lips.*

Ivy: Looking forward to testing out your skills.

Easton: Happy New Year, Ivy. Wish I really could kiss you tonight.

Ivy: Me too. Happy New Year.

. . .

Jan 2

Easton: It's been one week since I've seen you. Besides our phone calls and texts, my life feels very boring suddenly. What did you do to me?

Ivy: You really know how to make a girl blush. My life feels lame now too. What are we going to do about it?

Easton: Funny you should ask. We have a group coming through here from the fifth of the month until the nineteenth. What if I came to LA sometime after the twentieth?

The massive squeal that shot from Ivy's lips made heads at the busy TV station turn.

"Sorry," she offered from her place among the sea of desks. Well, five desks, to be exact. She set her gaze back on her phone as a rush of excitement filled her body.

Easton was coming to LA! It had been hard for Ivy to be patient since she returned home, but she sensed Easton needed to go at his own pace. He likely needed time to process the idea of dating anyone, let alone a woman from another state. But already he was talking about a trip out to see her. She could hardly believe it was true.

Ivy: I would love it if you came out here! In fact, I just now added it to my calendar and I've already dipped it in bronze. That makes it final, right?

Easton: If that's all it takes to make things final, consider yourself in Colorado by midnight. I'll write it on my planner now and bronze the crud out of it.

She stared at the text while her heart broke into a happy dance.

"Ivy, Nancy, could you ladies come into my office please?"

Ivy glanced up in time to see Marsha slip back into her office.

Nancy shot to a stand. "Coming!"

Ivy followed suit. "I wonder what this is all about?"

"You've got me." Nancy twirled a wad of gum around her finger as she led the way.

Ivy's mind shot back to the situation with Marsha and the woman's disappointment over Easton backing out. The mere recollection made her muscles tense. Had there been a new development?

The knot in her gut began to throb. A knot that had long since passed once Ivy broke the news. Sure, Marsha had been upset that Easton backed out, refusing to—in Ivy's words—do the interview or sign the contract, but she hadn't pushed the topic.

"Close the door," Marsha said once they stepped inside.

Ivy did just that as Nancy lowered herself into one of the white leather chairs across from Marsha's desk. Ivy took a seat beside her and tried not to look at the massive mural behind Marsha featuring a great white shark with razor sharp teeth.

"Nancy, please explain how you got hold of Easton Spark's interview and contract."

Ivy fought back a gasp as those words rearranged themselves in her head. The interview! *And* the contract too?

"Ivy and I upload our data into the same cloud," Nancy explained. "We know whose is whose, of course, and don't normally bother with one another's, but when Ivy didn't check in with us before Christmas, I figured she got caught in the storm, so I sent hers in for her." Nancy glanced over to Ivy. "For *you*, I should say." She shrugged innocently.

Ivy pulled in a shallow breath, the heated air like lava in her lungs. She wanted to think that Nancy wasn't innocent at all, but she couldn't possibly have known that Ivy planned to delete both files. Or that she'd made an agreement with Easton to say he'd changed his mind instead.

"So..." Marsha said, dragging out the word and resting her elbows on her desk. "Imagine my confusion, Ivy. Because earlier, you flew back to LA with news that Easton had changed his mind and that you *didn't* get the interview or signature at all."

It felt like fists were tightening around Ivy's throat. Was it her turn to speak yet? And if so, what would she possibly say for herself? She'd told a bold-faced lie and there was no getting around it.

"We take a few days off for the new year," Marsha continued, "and I step back into my office to see an email from Nancy that contains both of the files *you* said didn't exist."

Now. Now it was her turn. Another rush of fire-hot heat moved from her chest to her neck and then settled into her face. She could only fess up at this point and hope her explanation would save her.

"I'm...*very* sorry for not being upfront with you," Ivy started. "I *did* get the interview and signature, in the very beginning. But then after being with Easton all that time, he opened up to me and said that he *really* didn't want to do it and that he was just doing it for his sister because he lost a bet."

"So what?" Marsha sat up tall in her chair once more and

narrowed a hard look at her. "Do you know how many people get cold feet at the altar? Or nauseously nervous before a first date? Should we encourage everyone to simply cave to their fears, Ivy?"

She shook her head. "No."

"I say that to show that you weren't, in fact, doing *him* a favor at all. But that's beside the point. Because you don't work for Easton Sparks, you work for me. Not only was it *not* your job to cater to his misgivings, it was *completely* out of line and a breach of your employment contract." She drummed her fingers on the desk while her lips pinched shut.

Ivy dropped her gaze to the woman's manicured nails, feeling each audible clank like tiny stabs in her heart. The heat that had rushed to her face had officially gone south because suddenly her head was cased in a cool sweat.

"You can leave now, Nancy," Marsha said.

Nancy sucked the neglected wad of gum off her finger with an audible slurp. "Thank you."

Ivy kept her gaze locked on the desk while her traitorous coworker snuck out. Of *course* Nancy had to be the hero of the day, ruining everything for Ivy in the process. And what about Easton? Would Marsha make him hold up his end of the contract now that she had a signed copy? Ivy cursed that unyielding part of herself that, in her moments of rescue, thought only of getting the promotion. She'd risked draining her phone battery with no known way of recharging it and insisted also on uploading it to the storage cloud in the midst of a blizzard. Of course, that was specifically what she'd been paid to do. It's why she'd flown to Colorado in the first place, on the company's dime...

"Was there anything...inappropriate going on between you and Mr. Sparks?"

Whoa. "Inappropriate?" The echo came out in a squeak.

"Because if there was, I'd consider that to be an additional breach in your contract. Your job was to interview our potential bachelors for the show, not try to talk them out of it because you suddenly suffer from a fit of jealousy."

"That's not what happened," Ivy assured.

"I'd like you to pack your things, Ivy. You can either take an assistant position with the production crew downstairs—an obvious demotion—or you can seek employment elsewhere. What will it be?"

This couldn't be happening. Ivy shook her head, wishing it could somehow free her from the alternate realm she'd stumbled into. "I don't..."

"At least if you accept a position with the production crew, you'll have a chance of seeing Easton again before he enters the mansion."

Ivy felt her eyes widen in shock. This time there was no hiding the gasp. "You're going to make him do it?"

"Of *course* I'm going to make him do it. *You've* seen him."

Her heart hammered out one despairing beat after the next, each pressing hard against Ivy's ribs like an angry tide.

"We'd be crazy to let a specimen like that slip from our grip," Marsha was saying. "Besides, men who say they don't want to do it...they usually just want to be talked into it. Sometimes men need their ego stroked a little—*that* would have been the right thing to do. I assumed after all this time of working for me in this capacity you'd know that. So, what will it be?"

"The crew job," Ivy blurted. "Thank you." Tears pricked the corers of her eyes.

"Okay then," Marsha said. "Ask for Sally when you get downstairs. I believe you know her."

Yes, Ivy had trained Sally, in fact. She hurried to a stand and bolted for the door.

"Oh, and Ivy?" came Marsha once more.

Ivy looked over her shoulder from the doorway.

"This wasn't easy for me. I've always felt that you and I had something in common—a mutual respect and even love for these types of productions."

"I *do,*" she assured. "It helps people find love. What's better than that?"

Marsha held her gaze for a blink, seeming to test her sincerity. Ivy sensed the woman—as hard-nosed as she could be—was genuinely hurt by this. At last Marsha nodded, then turned her gaze out the window. "Please close the door on your way out."

Ivy dashed out, closed the door as Marsha instructed, and darted toward the lady's room. The rather large foyer, equipped with lounge chairs, magazines, and tissues, was the perfect place to unload the tears. Tears that were already breaking through.

They were going to force Easton to go on the show. Or slap him with a hefty lawsuit if he refused. And it was all her fault. Ivy needed to warn Easton, she knew that. She would, but first she had to get herself together.

CHAPTER 14

Jazz music hummed over Jessie's Diner as Easton took in his sister's response. Sure, he could have told Chantelle about Ivy and everything that happened before now, but the timing hadn't felt right.

"I have to say," Chantelle said with the shake of her head. "I'm really surprised. And impressed."

Easton squirmed beneath his sister's scrutinizing gaze. "Don't be. I still have no idea how this is going to work. I can't pick up and move to LA, and I doubt she'd be willing to leave California."

"It's only like a three-hour flight, isn't it?" she asked.

"Two and a half," he corrected, glancing out the window. Beyond the glass, a snow tractor moved about the distant parking lot while thick layers of bright snow heaped high in the curved shovel. "I'm looking at flights to head out there after our January group comes through."

"Hmm..." was all she replied.

It wasn't the sort of response he'd anticipated. Easton had known Chantelle from the time she was born; he knew how exuberant she could get over things like this. *Something's not right.*

Slowly then, his mind repeating the notion along the way, Easton moved his gaze back to the warm interior of the diner, first to the old oak table and paper placemats, then up to his sister.

His pulse jumped as he took in her expression—eyes dark and conflicted, her forehead and jaw tight with worry. Or even fear.

"What's wrong, Chantelle?" A painful push of anxiety shot through his form, tightening his limbs as memories rushed in, of times he'd seen that expression before. Moments she'd upset Mom or Dad, or on nights she feared one of their visitors might break into their room.

"Is it the baby? *What?*"

Chantelle shook her head and gripped onto the sides of the small table. "You said that Ivy agreed to *not* send the interview and contract, right?"

Where was she going with this? And just why was it causing her so much concern? "Right," he urged.

"Is it possible that she…*tricked* you somehow?"

This was not a direction he saw coming. Yet, as off base as her comment might be, the upset surging throughout his body multiplied.

"Why would you even suggest that?" Sure, he sounded angry now, but that's because he was. Chantelle hadn't even met Ivy. Who was she to make accusations? She was probably just upset that he was backing out of the bet.

"Ivy wasn't trying to *trick* me out of doing the show," he insisted. "In fact, it would have been *far* better for her career if I *had* done it. She probably lost a promotion over it."

But the look on his sister's face didn't change. The crease along her brow only deepened as she assessed him. Quietly. Painfully.

"Hey, if you're just ticked off because I backed out of the bet, get over it. If your *real* reason for wanting me to go on there was to help me find someone—mission accomplished, okay? I found someone that I can actually see a positive future with. You should be celebrating the fact, not…taking shots at the one woman I finally…let *in*."

"Trust me, Easton, I want to, but there's something you don't know." She shot a sideways glance toward the front of the café, guiding his attention to a small crowd gathered there.

He squinted to survey the scene, unable to guess at what the danger might be, when his phone started to ring. Easton's head swayed as he glanced at the screen. "It's Ivy."

Chantelle nodded as if she knew something. "Get it if you want, but I'm afraid she's been lying to you."

His thumb felt numb as he tapped the screen and pulled the device to his ear. "Ivy?"

"I'm so sorry, Easton," she said in a rush. "They found your interview and your waiver too. If you don't already know, they've landed in Denver and are headed your way."

He pressed the phone closer to his ear and searched the cluster of people at the entrance. "Who's they?"

"The recording crew for *Looking For Love*. Marsha's holding you to your contract, and there'll be repercussions if you don't follow through."

Easton turned a look on his sister. "You *knew* about this?"

Chantelle tipped her head apologetically, but Ivy answered through the line before his sister could. "*No!* Easton, I—"

"We have a special announcement, patrons," the owner, Jessie, declared, a small megaphone to her lips. She was heading his way with an entourage of gawkers and camera crew at her heels.

"How'd they know I'd be here?" he hissed under his breath.

Chantelle leaned over the table. "I told them, of course. They said you were selected for the show and this is the next step. They film your reaction."

"Easton?" Ivy came through the line.

Fury flared within him. Chantelle was right—Ivy *had* betrayed him. All to get her stupid promotion? His jaw clenched hard. "Man," he breathed. "I really am a sucker, aren't I? It's been nice doing *business* with you, Ivy." Easton pressed the small power button with more strength than necessary and fisted the device as the crowd approached.

"We have one of America's most eligible bachelors in our midst, friends," Jessie continued as she neared. "Right here at table number six."

Easton straightened as a man with a wide-lens camera propped on his shoulder came into view. This could not be happening. A woman with an identical-looking camera locked her lens on his sister.

Jessie nodded toward Chantelle expectantly, as if it was *her* turn to carry on the rest of the cringe-worthy chaos.

"Surprise," she squeaked, her face red with all the upset and worry she felt.

Easton couldn't take the glare off his face as he eyed the

expectant crowd, one intruder after the next, hungry for a taste of the action.

Chantelle cleared her throat, and all heads turned her way. "You got picked," she said, forcing a pathetic looking smile. "For the, um...*Looking For Love* show," she added.

Suddenly the female with the camera tipped her head away from the lens and looked at Chantelle. "Let's try that again with a little more enthusiasm. And remember to add that he leaves today."

"*Today*?" Easton's brow furrowed. His jaw clenched.

"The producers like to isolate contestants for a few days to keep them from the media before they enter the mansion," Chantelle explained. "We brought in Max as a replacement at the center. Things there will be fine."

"Okay, let's go back to the announcement, please," the lady behind the lens instructed once more.

Were they kidding? Easton turned a look over his shoulder, desperate for a way out. The aisle leading toward the entrance would be blocked for days. But, if he recalled correctly, there was an emergency exit in the rear beside the kitchen, just beyond the men's room.

And as luck would have it, the booth behind him was clear.

At once he flung his arm along the back of the booth and hoisted a foot onto the bench. "If you'll excuse me..." Hunching on the bench now, Easton hurdled the divider and landed on the bench behind him. He dodged the hanging light in time to land in the empty part of the aisle. Onlookers sat in booths, gawking as whispers broke out over the crowd.

Darkness cased him in the narrow hallway as he strode toward the glowing green sign. A small child and her mom exited the ladies room, but Easton breezed right past them with ease.

"Where's he going?" a little voice came.

Anywhere but here. Who cared what they made of it? Let them think he was rushing to the men's room, nauseous or camera shy from all the attention. Let them think he was making some cowardly escape. Easton didn't care *what* they assumed. Max was replacing him for the upcoming group at the center? Great. He'd make his escape alright, and Easton didn't care if they brought on an entire search party; he'd disappear until he wanted to be found.

With that thought, Easton shoved open the dark exit door and made his escape.

CHAPTER 15

Ivy released a deep sigh as she stared at her new office surroundings. It seemed impossible that three days had gone by without a word from Easton Sparks. His sister, Chantelle, had reached out to her shortly after he'd angrily ended their call. With Ivy's permission, Marsha had given Chantelle the number, which had been, in some ways, a saving grace. At least Ivy could talk to someone who cared about him too. Who was concerned for his well-being.

During their rather lengthy phone conversation, Chantelle explained what happened at the diner. *He just got up, stomped into the other booth, and went right out the exit.*

Ivy couldn't help but play that horrific moment again and again. *...was nice doing business with you, Ivy.* She kept waiting for the recollection to lose its punch, but it never did. It seemed to grow more powerful instead, the mere recollection zapping every sense of peace Ivy owned. He actually thought she'd betrayed him, that this was all about business to her. That was the worst part of all.

It felt as if electric eels were swarming throughout her insides, bumping into vessels, crashing against nerves, and disrupting the rhythm of her heart. A heart that felt like it was breaking into a trillion tiny pieces.

What if Easton never talked to her again? She couldn't even fathom the thought.Chantelle had done her best to put Ivy's mind at ease, assuring her that Easton would come around. He was a man who needed his space. He was quiet, private and, his sister went on to say through tears, *totally* unsuited for a reality TV show. She now regretted forcing it on him as she had.

But at least Chantelle, unlike Easton, had given Ivy the chance to explain. It was the one peace of mind she had. Easton may have his mind set on never talking to Ivy again, but he *would* talk to Chantelle, and Chantelle could set things straight.

Unless he was looking for a way out.

That was a very real possibility as well. One she didn't like thinking about.

The Nature Rehab Center's January program started that morning and, as Chantelle predicted, Easton hadn't shown.

She glanced down at her phone to reread her recent text thread with Chantelle.

Ivy: I really thought he'd show up today. He loves his job so much, it seems like something he'd never purposely miss.

Chantelle: Yeah, but he knew I had arranged for a replacement so he could go on the show. I wish now I wouldn't have told him. He'd definitely be here otherwise.

But he wasn't, and now they'd be left to wonder where he'd gone off to. And for who knew how long? Nature specialist as he was, Easton could probably live a long happy life in a yurt or a snow hut, with only the wolves and wildlife as his friends.

Would he hide out in the wilderness from one season to the next, become some sort of caveman, all to dodge a fate he couldn't face? Thank heavens Easton had Chantelle. He loved her too much to disappear completely, Ivy knew that much. And he'd want to be around when the baby was born.

But where did *she* fit into the equation? And what about the potential lawsuit he faced for bailing? Marsha wasn't exactly the vindictive type, but she was known to get what she wanted one way or another, and she wasn't above getting her hands dirty.

If only Nancy hadn't sent those files to Marsha, if only Ivy hadn't sent them to the company cloud back on that snowy day, she and Easton might have really stood a chance.

Was she just fooling herself to believe he would ever be able to fall in love? Not just in love in general, which seemed a great enough feat in itself, but in love with *her*. That, among all the madness of the last few days, seemed impossible to her now. One could only suspend disbelief for so long before it all came crashing down.

And as Ivy thought back on the time she'd spent with him, whether wrapped in his embrace, dancing about the yurt, or enjoying his passionate kiss, she was glad she had the memories to cherish.

She tugged open her desk drawer and retrieved one of the ornaments he'd made. While preparing to leave the yurt, they'd decided to divide the handmade ornaments in two, each taking half. Ivy had scattered them about, hanging one of the twig crosses he'd made on her rearview, and another on her bedpost. Between the rooms in her house, the drawers in her desk, and her car's glovebox and mirror, she was greeted several times a day with the lovely trinkets that put a smile on her face and a skip in the beat of her heart.

But over the last few days, the items seemed to haunt her instead. To remind her of what she'd *almost* had.

A buzz came from her desk phone, and Ivy wasted no time snatching it up. "Hello?"

"I need to pick your brain about Easton," Marsha said. "The media's buzzing about it, and I need answers."

Oh, great. The media?

"Come up to my office, please."

Ivy straightened up. "Okay." A burst of encouragement pushed through her. Perhaps Marsha was looking for a way to let Easton out of his contract. Perhaps he'd gotten in touch with them. She hurried to her feet and headed toward the elevators. She was halfway to Marsha's office before she realized she'd left her phone behind.

An irrational sense of fear took over at the thought of missing a call from Easton. *Stop it, Ivy. You're probably the last person he'd call right now.*

The sad truth of that statement made her eyes sting. It made her heart feel like it was bleeding suddenly, from a very raw and aching gash. Had she ever really had a chance with Easton? And if so, were those chances as squashed as she believed they were?

Marsha stood next to her open door, moving aside to let Ivy enter as she arrived.

"Thank you for coming," she said, voice even and calm. The woman motioned for Ivy to take a seat.

She did, watching as Marsha walked to the front of her desk

and leaned against it, arms folded over her chest. The woman surveyed her for a moment before speaking up.

"I talked with Chantelle again this afternoon. She told me that Easton confided in her before the crew showed up." Marsha snatched a stapled stack of papers off her desk, flipped a few pages, and stared at the image beneath—a close up of Easton.

Oh man. Ivy hadn't seen his face since they'd said goodbye. In her mind, yes, but in print, right before her eyes…

Ivy couldn't take it. She clenched her eyes shut and dropped her gaze to the floor, but it was too late. All she could see was his head shot—no doubt provided by Chantelle. An outdoor photo, of course, where Easton was in his true form. He wore a navy blue shirt. She hadn't seen that color on him yet. In the photo, it did wonderful things for his olive skin tone.

The smile, on the other hand, she'd witnessed that several times. Soft chimes of Christmas music played out in her mind. She could see that very smile, beaming and wide as he danced with her in the firelight, the scent of pine heavy in the air.

Ivy's hands shot to her face as an emotional blizzard tore through her. Her lip quivered as she fought to hold it back. Fought, and failed.

The welled-up tears trickled down her cheeks. There was nowhere else for them to go. And the pent-up sobs, to her absolute horror, broke free. That one glimpse of his photo unleashing all of the heartache and lost hope she'd had trapped in her five-and-a-half-foot frame.

"I'm sorry," she managed through the tears. "I just haven't seen him since we said goodbye. And that face…" She shook her head.

"It *is* quite the face," Marsha agreed. "In a way, this is his own fault. If he didn't have such a ridiculous appeal, I might have let him out of his contract."

Ivy laughed from the comment, then broke into tears again.

Marsha nudged her arm with a tissue box. "Here," she said, "you might not know this about me, but I'm a romantic at heart. My drive for success on these shows is not all about the money and ratings. But without those things, we don't have much of a show, do we?"

Ivy snatched two tissues from the box and blew her nose into one of them. "I've got to get myself together," she said. "I don't think I've cried like this in front of anyone in my entire life. Not since I was a little kid anyway." She'd been teased by her siblings for crying—a fact that had taught her to choke back tears at a young age.

"Listen, Ivy. I took an early liking to you because you're a hard worker, and you seemed to respect these productions, which are often dismissed as silly or irrelevant. I'd like to give you a second chance."

Ivy glanced up in surprise and sniffed. "You would?"

"I'd also like to present an offer to Easton. But I can't do that until I know what happened between the two of you." Marsha chuckled wryly. "I don't need *all* of the little details, of course, but if I'm going to consider giving Easton a way out, and if I'm going to excuse *your* part in the matter, I need to get the gist. It will help me combat any tabloid gossip as well."

Ivy couldn't get herself to worry about the tabloids, because big spots of hope were sprouting deep in her chest. Her shoulders rose as she nodded and pulled in a breath. "Okay."

Marsha moved to the chair beside her and turned it so they

were face to face. Marsha leaned in then, the posture mimicking moments Ivy had with her teenaged friends back in high school.

"Now then," she said, sparks of delight dancing in her green eyes. "Tell me what happened while you were snowed-in with Easton Sparks."

CHAPTER 16

"Hand me a Diet Coke, will you, Tim?" Chantelle sat beside Easton on the sofa before the big screen TV, resting a hand over her pregnant belly.

"Sure thing," her husband, Tim, said. "Easton, you want anything? Water, beer, moonshine peaches?"

Easton grimaced and paused, the strange comment—along with the fact that Tim's face was actually someone else's face—making him realize that he wasn't where he thought he was, where his dreaming *mind told him he was. He was sleeping in his tent among a spread of red rock petroglyphs in Nevada.*

"Sure," Easton told Tim anyway. "I'll take a water."

"Welcome to our very first episode of Looking For Love,*" came the announcer from the TV. Why that announcer looked exactly like Easton's sixth grade teacher, he wasn't sure. But he went along with it. May as well hurry and get that water; he was parched.*

"We have an announcement for you folks at home," the host continued. "Due to a family emergency, one of our bachelorettes was

unable to participate, leaving our twenty-five bachelors with just four candidates. But never fear—our producer handed the honor to one of our very own staff here at the station, and what a beauty she is. Let's have her come out now, folks. Give a warm welcome to the beautiful Miss Ivy Ingles!"

The curtain parted.

Ivy appeared in the spotlight, a glittering dress casing her curvy figure. Appreciative cat calls rang out from the crowd.

"Pick me, Ivy!" hollered a man in a suit and tie. Wait, that wasn't just any man. That was David Beckham. And he wasn't wearing a suit and tie anymore. In fact, he wasn't wearing much clothing at all. Tattoos cased his arms and part of his bare chest as he strode onto the stage, took Ivy in his arms, and dipped her back for a kiss before the crowd.

Easton's eyes shot open in a bout of horror. The gasp that pulled from his throat echoed within the small tent. So did the rapid breaths that followed. He shoved a palm against his thumping heart, willing it to slow. Willing the nagging ache to subside. Talk about a nightmare.

He dropped his face in his hands and sighed. If Easton was going to be tormented by his dreams, at least he could've dreamt about his and Ivy's time in the yurt. Sure, he'd wake up miserable and aching and missing her even more, if that was possible, but at least he'd get to relive some of their moments—the sound of her cute little laugh, the feel of her warm and silky form in his arms, the tempting taste of her incredible kiss. The last thing he needed was to think about Ivy kissing another man, for crying out loud.

He raked his hands through his hair, certain this was a certified form of torture—being ripped away from the woman he was falling in love with, only to have her betray him within days of their goodbye.

It was a real-life nightmare. Heartache was part of the whole dating game—there was no getting around it—but Easton couldn't help but think his heart hurt worse than the norm, if there was such a thing. He'd finally opened himself to someone, to the idea of having a life together even, as premature as it might have been. Not on purpose, either. It was just that Ivy had a way of making him see the possibilities in a whole new light. Outcomes that *didn't* result in ruin. And now, without Ivy, he feared he'd lost that perspective for good.

Similar thoughts clung to his mind as Easton packed up and retrieved his supplies. He'd spent five and a half days in Nevada's Valley of Fire National Park. And while he might end up staying the entire month, he wanted to check in with Chantelle.

A list of things had prodded at him over the last few days. Normally, it didn't bother him to be without service. But this time, after he'd taken off without notice, left his sister in the dark about his whereabouts—not to mention stranded with an expectant camera crew at the diner—Easton's conscience was getting the better of him.

She deserved it, he assured himself. And that might be true. In Easton's mind, both Chantelle and Ivy deserved what came of their attempts to force him onto a dating reality TV show—one meant to end in a proposal for those who found love within the short timeframe, no less. Of course, that idea didn't sound as ludicrous to him now as it had before. Just three days in a yurt with Ivy was enough to have Easton changing everything he thought he believed about love.

With his tent and supplies stuffed into his backpack, Easton headed toward the main trail. The sun was bright, the air was warm, but the frigid ache in his heart remained as he trekked the mile-long walk to his Jeep. His phone waited for him there, a fact that only now had Easton wondering what he might have missed. A lame explanation from Ivy? A concerned message from Chantelle?

The thought caused a spark of fear to kindle within him. What if something had happened with the baby? He'd never forgive himself for not being there if it had. Similar thoughts caused Easton to move faster towards his Jeep.

If Ivy had left messages for him, what exactly would they say? Would she explain that missing out on the promotion was too great a sacrifice? Or would she skip the repentant act altogether and tell him all was fair in love and war? Thoughts like those made Easton want to stop in his tracks, head back to his camping spot, and set up his tent again without bothering to check in at all.

But he wouldn't do that.

He had some music to face before he could hibernate once more. He'd get chewed out from Chantelle for not touching base sooner. He was probably already getting threats of legal action by the station for backing out of his contract. He might even catch slack from a few angry parents over the last-minute staff replacement at the center. Not that Max wasn't a suitable replacement. Heck, the guy had been one of the first teens to go through the course five years ago. And now he was stepping up and changing lives in return.

Changing lives. The statement forced his mind right back to Ivy. She'd changed his entire outlook if nothing else. And then she betrayed him.

Once in the Jeep, the door wide open to let the fresh air in, Easton turned on his phone and watched the messages filter in. Three from Chantelle; he'd expected those. Two texts from Ivy popped up next. He'd been expecting those too, but the sight made his heart hiccup all the same. A burning sensation followed, as if the organ had been soaked in acid.

A few texts from an unknown number appeared beneath hers. He moved his thumb back up to hover over Ivy's name, but he couldn't get himself to open the thread just yet; whether she'd sent him a genuine apology or a list of lies, he wasn't sure he could stomach the added torment it might bring. He clicked on Chantelle's instead.

Chantelle: *Please call me.*

Chantelle: *This isn't what it looks like. You need to call me right now.*

"No," he replied aloud, irritation pushing through him at the memory of those horrible moments in the diner. Easton might have felt ready to address what he'd walked away from, but now that the option was before him, the access line right in his palm, the desire fled faster than a fox on a hunt. He glanced down at her final text.

Chantelle: *If you won't call me, you at least need to call Ivy and give her a chance to explain. You owe her that.*

Easton rolled his eyes. Now the two were in cahoots?

He clicked on the thread of texts from the unknown caller next, half wondering if it'd be Ivy texting from another phone in hopes to get a response. It wasn't.

Unknown Number: *This is Marsha Langston, producer of* Looking For Love. *As it stands, the station has a hefty case against you for breaking your contract. One that could take down the rehab facility—I'd hate to see that happen. But I've got an offer for you. A way out of your contract without repercussion. I'll even throw in a hefty donation to the facility. Please call right away as this offer is time sensitive.*

"Great." Easton shook his head and groaned. He didn't feel like making any deals. But how could he forgive himself if the rehab center took a hit for his mistake? And was that how he viewed all of this—as a mistake? If he could take the whole thing back, his agreement to follow through with the interview, all those hours with Ivy in the yurt, would he do it?

He moved onto the next text by the same number.

Unknown Number: *Marsha Langston again. What did you do to my poor Ivy? She burst into tears at the sight of your photo.*

The words were a sharp punch to the gut. One that had Easton bracing himself too late against the pain. Maybe betraying him hadn't been such an easy thing for her. At least there was that. If she did, in fact, get emotional at the sight of his image, it said she *did* have real feelings for him after all. But had he doubted that? Not with any sincerity, he hadn't. But in the end she cared more about her job than she did him.

Still, it went beyond that. Because the betrayal would send Easton into a situation where he'd be, by name of the show, looking for love. Just the mere thought of Ivy going on the show like she had in his dream sent fire-hot darts through his heart. He'd do anything to *prevent* such a thing. That's what hurt most of all. The idea that she not only didn't mind the thought of him pursuing other women, she was the one who'd sentenced him to that fate.

So was she having misgivings? Did she regret doing what she'd promised *not* to do? With his insides in knots, a pounding in his head, and a nagging ache in his heart, Easton scrolled down to read the next text from the show's producer.

Unknown Number: *Marsha again. Listen, I don't know if you're playing hardball or if you're stuck in a klondike cave like some boy scout on the run. You had misgivings after signing the contract. That's understandable. But forget that for a minute. If you care about Ivy at all, if you feel there was really something between the two of you, you need to stop running, stop hiding, and talk to her face-to-face. Or were you just faking the whole time? Hoping to seduce her so she'd hide the interview and the contract you later regretted signing?*

His stomach lurched. A curse fell from his lips. "Why'd she have to bring Ivy into it?" And the accusation too. *Seduce* her—was she crazy? And to accuse him of faking the whole time. This meant Ivy told the producer that they'd gotten…close.

Great.

Every physical part of him was in turmoil. From the rattling rhythm of his heart to the sharp and tearing pain in his gut. And just what was happening to his head? It felt fuzzy suddenly. And…and…

Easton turned sideways toward the open door on the driver seat, lowered his elbows to his knees, and dropped his head to catch some slow and steady breaths. How was he going to fix this? If Marsha was convinced he'd seduced Ivy to keep her from sending in his contract, could Ivy be thinking along those same lines? But that would be ridiculous. *She* was the one who'd offered to not send it. As a *Christmas* gift, no less.

Some gift. And what now, she'd turned around and claimed he'd seduced her into withholding it? Now he *really* didn't want to read Ivy's texts. This was even worse than he thought.

He tossed a glance over his shoulder. Upon opening the

Jeep, Easton had thrown his items inside before checking his messages. Perhaps, subconsciously, he'd hoped to find something that explained everything away. Sure, he hadn't read Ivy's explanation yet, but he didn't need to now. Marsha's accusation said it all. He ticked off the offenses in his head one by one.

She'd sent in the contract after saying she wouldn't.

She'd sent in the video after claiming she'd delete it.

And now, she was blaming him for her delay in handing the stuff over. All so she could get her precious little promotion.

The list was proof that things had ended in disaster just like he'd feared. They'd just ended a whole lot sooner than he imagined. Another bout of disappointment pushed through him. He'd halfway hoped that the messages on his phone—the ones he'd gladly avoided for the last four days—might inspire him to go home after all. As it stood, even Marsha's threats weren't enough to lure him back. So things really were over with him and Ivy.

As much as the realization stung, Easton detected hints of relief among the pain. The greater agony, perhaps, was the struggle of making a relationship work. Trying to pursue something that was destined to end in ruin.

But accepting that it was over….well, it meant things would be easier now. Less messy. Less…*risky,* an inner voice filled in. The word made him feel like a coward. But so what if he was? He'd be a comfortable coward, safe from all the turmoil relationships brought. And who had he been fooling? Had Easton really believed he could change after all this time? And how absurd had it been for him to fall for a woman so thoroughly in just a few short days?

He shook his head. "Ridiculous." The mere recognition

brought Easton one step closer to the man he used to be, and he'd be lying if he said it didn't feel good.

With a bit of satisfaction, Easton climbed out of the Jeep, taking his gear along with him, and moved to put the phone back in the glovebox. Not that that was necessary; he wouldn't have cell service back at the campsite anyway. May as well keep it with him.

Yet as he walked away from his Jeep, away from the mess he'd decided *not* to address for now, the satisfaction he'd felt a moment ago fled. Loneliness seeped into its place. Cold, dark, and hollow. Guilt slunk in too. Shouldn't he just read what Ivy sent him? He didn't have to respond, did he?

In fact, he'd force himself *not* to respond right away. Even better, he'd sleep on it—wait until the next day to send any reply. That way, he wouldn't say anything he might regret. Yeah, that was good.

So, he'd do it. He'd see what Ivy had to say for herself, and then he'd go right back to his campsite.

Easton flicked his thumb over the screen to get back to his texts. And there it was, Ivy's simple three-letter name. The affection he felt at the sight of it made his heart cry out once more. A desperate yearning that swelled with each aching thump.

No replying today, he reminded himself. He tapped the screen over her name and read.

Ivy: *Easton, I'm not the one who sent in your contract. My coworker, Nancy, sent it, along with your interview, while I was gone. Please call and let me explain. I don't want you to go on the show either, but there's nothing I can do.*

Easton let that bomb rumble through him, the commotion

causing the layers he'd built in his mind to crumble. He shoved the phone back in his pocket and walked on, willing the sweat casing his face to hurry and cool against the breeze, but it wasn't. Another step more and he tugged the phone from his pocket and reread the message.

"Not the one who sent it in?"

Keep walking, Easton. That was the deal. But there was another message from her he wanted to read first.

Ivy: *Please, Easton. I'm sick to my stomach. Please call and let me hear your voice. Call and let me explain. I don't want to lose what we have.*

Another explosion rocked through him, displacing all the thoughts in his head. Why in heavens name *wouldn't* he call her? Maybe there really was a good explanation for the whole thing.

He gulped and, with a shaky hand, hovered his thumb over the icon at the top of the screen. The one that would call Ivy with one tap. A wave of something that felt an awful lot like fear pushed through him.

Just do it, Easton.

He did. One simple tap.

Another gulp slunk down his throat as he put it on speaker and waited for it to ring. It didn't. Instead, a machine picked up. One of those automated recordings saying the mailbox was full.

Relief clashed with torment as he thumped the disconnect icon harder than necessary and shoved the phone back in his pocket. He stayed like that, mid-stride, as the torment won. Loving someone—or *falling* in love, as he was—was terrible. Why did anyone do it? Even if they did fix things now, even if Ivy had a perfectly good explanation, did he really want to get sucked in so deep that he couldn't get out next time? What if this was his only chance to...to clear her out of his mind somehow?

The phone buzzed in his pocket, and Easton was quick to retrieve it. He anxiously tapped the screen. Was Ivy returning his call so soon?

No. It was another text from Marsha Langston.

Unknown Number: *The countdown is on. You've got until the end of the night to accept my offer. My very generous offer, I should say. Do everyone a favor and take care of this situation. It will only get worse if you ignore it.*

The end of the night, huh? Did that mean the show's premier would air that evening? Is that why it'd be too late after that? Easton didn't actually know when the start date was. Not that it mattered. He hated threats, and he didn't like being pushed around either. Besides, he'd made himself an agreement, hadn't he?

Yes, he had. He'd told himself he would *not* respond to anything until tomorrow. Sure, he'd tried to call Ivy after getting her text, but that was a mere moment of weakness. He was stronger now. And determined to let Marsha Langston's deadline pass before he reached out.

With that, Easton powered off his phone, secured his gear, and headed back to his campsite.

CHAPTER 17

Ivy stared down at the small invite in her hand. Marsha had become very generous since their discussion about Easton the other day. Not only had she given Ivy her job back, she'd given her four premier tickets to tonight's live production of *Looking For Love.* To prepare Ivy and her guests for the event, she'd gifted her and her guests a full-day spa treatment, lunch in the Spa's Korean eatery included.

As her guests, Ivy had chosen her sister Jackie and her sisters-in-law Taya and Joelle. Already, they'd spent hours in the women's bath house, enjoying body scrubs, facials, and foot rubs. They'd moved on to the steam room next, then hit several of the mineral heated huts on the way to lunch.

As if all of this wasn't enough, Ivy had received yet another invitation from Marsha, courtesy of the waitress who'd delivered their food—oversized bowls of ramen noodles with boiled eggs, wontons, and egg rolls.

Jackie leaned over her as she took the card and opened it. "What does it say?"

Ivy read it aloud. "To finish this day of luxury, and to prepare you for tonight's premier, I've provided a selection of gowns for you and your guests to choose from. They're waiting at the famous Hair and Now Salon, where hair and makeup specialists await you."

A unified squeal broke out over the table. "This is amazing, Ivy," Taya said. "She must really value you as an assistant."

"Seriously," Joelle added. "I'm glad I'm not further along," she said, giving her small belly a pat. "Already this day has been like a dream. And now we get to pick out formal gowns and get our hair and makeup done? I wish I had *your* job."

Ivy grinned and set her eyes back on the card where Marsha's signature was scrawled at the bottom. She couldn't help but think the woman had something up her sleeve. She only wished it had something to do with Easton. It wouldn't though. As big and broad as Ivy's imagination might stretch, she couldn't construct a scenario that would let Easton out of his contract. Beyond that, he'd have to actually show up first. And who knew when that would happen?

"Do you think Easton's going to be there?" Jackie might have been the one to pose the question, but there was a collective interest among the table, evident in the way Taya and Joelle leaned in over their food.

Taya, Danny's wife, skillfully guided her noodles to her lips with a pair of chopsticks. Ronny's wife, Joelle—also seated across from Ivy—did the same.

"I doubt it," Ivy said. "The guy knows how to live off the land. He's probably been off the radar ever since he walked out."

"I wonder what will happen when he finally gets your texts," Joelle said.

Jackie piped up. "Once he figures out that Ivy's not the one who handed that stuff in, he's going to freak out, call her the second he reads it, and beg for her forgiveness."

"I seriously doubt that," Ivy said.

"Why do you doubt it?" Taya challenged. "If he's as great as you think he is, that's *exactly* what he'll do."

Why did she doubt it? Because no one had ever fought for her before.

"When Dad messed up with Mom," Jackie started, "he got in his squad car to speed right past traffic jams to get to her, then got down on one knee and proposed."

"They were in a fight at the time?" Ivy asked. "I don't remember that part of the story."

"That's because they leave that part out," Jackie assured.

Taya leaned further in. "When I was ticked off at Danny one time," she said in a whisper, "he walked right out of a final exam to find me on campus and make it right."

"My old roommates will never forget the gesture Ronny made for missing my Nana's funeral. Flowers for *days.*"

A mean ache sank deep into Ivy's chest at the topic. Here, she'd finally managed to get some recognition about her job. Admiration, even, which felt great. It's what she'd wanted all these years. But now, with talk of grand gestures by the men who loved the women sitting at the table with her, Ivy realized she'd fall short in that department no matter *what* she achieved at her job.

No accomplishment *she* made would offer what these guys

had—a man who'd put a ring on her finger and swear his life to her.

"Well," she said, wishing she could shed the iron cloud descending over her head, "whatever happens tonight, it's going to be a lot of fun to watch. Two of the men I interviewed will be on the show tonight."

"Two, without counting Easton?" Jackie asked.

Ivy nodded. "Yep. The gambler from Vegas and the football player from Arizona."

"Would you *die* if Easton was there and he actually went onto the show?" Joelle asked.

Taya gave her arm a swat. "Hush, don't say things like that. He already refused to go on the show because he's got feelings for Ivy."

"Well, he's got a big objection to the whole set up, actually," Ivy corrected, heart still stinging from the idea of Easton in that mansion with five eligible bachelorettes. Women that men would compete for, fight for, speed onto a traffic-ridden interstate for.

"Yeah, but he likes you too," Taya insisted.

Ivy looked down at her uneaten food. Was this what her life would be like ten years from now? She'd still be Marsha's assistant, enjoying a few perks from her boss with the girls, then go home to an empty house while they returned to their families?

Tears clouded her eyes at the thought.

"We better hurry and finish our food, guys," Jackie blurted. Her tone sounded so urgent that Ivy started digging into her soup as well. She didn't want to go to the show tonight on an empty stomach. But a few bites into her food, Ivy felt a small pat on her leg from her sister.

A soothing one that said Jackie saw the pain she was in. That she was sorry for it. And that she'd provided a distraction to take the focus off of her. Ivy placed a hand over Jackie's and gave it a squeeze. Thank heavens for sisters.

Tonight, it was very unlikely that Ivy would see Easton, which was a heartbreaking fact in itself. But even worse was the fact that—if he *did* show—Easton would give a live interview for two minutes tops before heading into a mansion where five women would try everything in their power to get a proposal out of him.

There was no third option. But at least one thing could be said. Ivy might go home alone once the evening was through, but whatever the hours might bring, whatever the night might reveal, she'd have her sisters by her side.

CHAPTER 18

Nausea rolled through Easton as he tossed from his shoulder onto his back.

Ivy hadn't sent in the contract. Her coworker had.

He clenched his eyes shut tighter and shrugged onto his other side. Napping in the middle of the day had never been his specialty, but Easton needed the sleep. He'd had hardly any rest since the time he'd arrived, and his mind was starting to slip. Besides, if he could manage to ignore the daylight and fall fast asleep, perhaps he could avoid the temptation to leave the campsite and do something...something the stubborn part of him didn't want to do.

Do everyone a favor and take care of the situation by tonight. Has to be tonight.

Easton groaned and gave his stow-away pillow a couple of shoves at each corner, hoping a little comfort might lull him into sleep.

What did you do to poor Ivy? She burst into tears at the sight of your picture.

Please call, Easton. I'm sick to my stomach. I don't want to lose what we have.

Lose what they had. That was the biggest enigma of all. *That* was the unsolvable mystery that had kept him up every night since he left. Which said something since *this*—sleeping in tents beneath the sky—this used to be his haven, his happy place, his refuge no matter the storm.

Now it seemed his only refuge was in thoughts of Ivy. In recollections of holding her in his arms. Of kissing her silky lips. Of laughing at her family tales and goofy jokes.

His heart thundered as—vision after vision, memory after memory—the torment multiplied. Ivy's solemn text played out in the sound of her voice in his mind, a prodding, pressing repeat that had him shrugging onto his stomach and forcing the pillow over his head.

Don't want to lose what we have.

Don't want to lose what we have.

But now it's too late, Easton, he could hear her saying. *You won't even listen to what I have to say. You're punishing me for something I didn't even do. Thanks for proving that the other men in my life were right all along. Thanks for making it that much harder to trust.*

Another groan tore through him as he sat up and reached for the bag at his side. The zipper was cool beneath his touch. He grabbed the small tab and tugged it open, then pulled the phone from its pouch. It took a moment for it to power on, but once it did, Easton saw that it was only 4:00.

This day was never going to end. Sure, the sun had already

started to set, but was he really willing to stick it out for the whole night? He'd promised himself to sleep on it. *It* being the messages he'd gotten from Ivy and Marsha Langston. But if *sleeping* was not in the cards, how could he achieve that?

His mind must have been one step ahead of him. Already Easton was reaching for his socks and shoes. He shoved into them before unzipping his tent and climbing out. He was about to pack up all of his gear when he thought better of it. *Call first.*

A red-tailed hawk cawed overhead, drawing his attention to the colorful sunset in the distance. The reflection of light caused the pink formations to glow nearly red—it was the Valley of Fire, after all.

Ivy would like this, he decided. It was beautiful. He could acknowledge the fact easily enough, but he couldn't enjoy the sight for himself. Not at a time like this.

Easton watched the bars on his phone, waiting until they said he could call. Getting up and out of the tent had quelled his anxiety at first. But now, with each additional step he took, his nerves became more and more agitated. The parking area was in sight now. May as well try to make a call.

Yet just as he moved to click on the screen, a text came in from his sister.

Chantelle: *Thought you better see this for yourself.*

It took a moment for the image to pop up, but once it did, a spark of amusement flashed through him. It was a magazine article of some sort, a tabloid probably, with the title "Runaway Bachelor" on the front. Less amusing was the photo they had of him. Some picture taken at the rehab center a few years back.

If this was supposed to pack some sort of punch, it had failed by a long shot. Easton would rather be some flash in the pan runaway bachelor who would—by any stretch of the imagination—fizzle out in days than have to go on that horrible show and make a fool of himself.

But then another image came up. It was a shot taken of the article spread inside.

A curse fell from his lips. And then another as he looked over the photo they'd printed of Ivy. "They had to drag her into it," he muttered.

In the photo, Ivy was sitting up to a table, a plastic lobster bib tied around her neck, readying to take a fake bite from the shiny red lobster on her plate.

How they'd managed to find a less-than-flattering photo of a woman so obviously beautiful was beyond him. And *why* in heavens name would they do it? They probably assumed a woman who looked like her didn't have an insecurity in the world. Little did they know...

A groan rumbled in his chest as he scrutinized the image some more.

Reluctantly, Easton read the small print beneath it.

Rumors have it that Ivy Ingles, assistant to Looking For Love's *producer Marsha Langston, got caught in a blizzard with this gorgeous bachelor while filming his interview. Lucky girl! I'm sure he knows how to keep a woman warm—just look at him.*

The strange thing is that the interview never made it to Langston. Until Ivy's co-worker sent it in.

Hmmm... sounds fishy to us.

Was this blonde-haired lobster-eater so obsessed with the handsome hunk that she tried to keep him off the show? Was she hoping he'd pick the pauperess over the princesses he'd find in the show's castle-like mansion?

We think so! What do you think?

What kind of slanted garbage was this? How did Ivy get made out to look like that? *He* was the one who'd run off. And he was also the one who'd allowed her to withhold the interview.

His fist clenched so tight it hurt. His jaw did the same. It felt like fire was racing through his veins. This was an outrage. Ivy's worst nightmare come to life and magnified a million times over. His mind raced for a way to fix it. To somehow champion Ivy in a way big enough for...for everyone who saw this ridiculous article to be set straight. For the slimy creator of the magazine to eat his or her words by way of public embarrassment.

This wasn't about Easton dodging a lawsuit or a TV show anymore, this was about him defending a woman who didn't deserve any of this. And he'd make it his life goal to do that very thing.

But first...

Easton exed out of the text thread, scrolled down to Ivy's name, and pressed the call icon. Why call Marsha about making a deal when all he could think about was Ivy? He had to apologize. He had to make it right. He had to...had to at least hear her voice.

He put the device on speaker, a bit of déjà vu coming on as it went straight to voicemail once more, the same automated message that said her mailbox was too full. Only after seeing the article, that made more sense; probably a bunch of messages from vicious paparazzi. Should he text her instead? May as well. He could barely contain the anger coursing through him as he tapped out a message instead.

Easton: *I'm so sorry, Ivy. I was a jerk to take off without letting you explain. I got angry. And scared. But I don't want to lose you either.*

He decided not to mention the article. If she hadn't seen it for herself, the last thing he'd want to do is make her aware of it. He read over the text once before hitting send, then paced back and forth along the dirt ground. "Where are you, Ivy? And what's the deal with your phone?"

A new level of desperation tore through him. One that had him dying to drive straight to LA. It would only take him, what, five or six hours?

The red hawk circled overhead once more, crying out its lonely call. Easton related. If he could verbally cry out, loud enough to reach Ivy, he would, right there with the dry rocky land surrounding him. And once he found her, he'd apologize for leaving her in the fray of his mess. For making her the subject of ugly, inaccurate gossip with no one to defend her.

And then, he mused, once they'd made up, he'd bring her out here to enjoy the sunset. And he'd see what kind of dorky fun facts they could exchange about wildlife and petroglyphs and... and the unexplainable connection between a man and a woman in love. That was a topic he knew little about. But his fascination for it was rampant now. Because there was no real explanation for it. No reason he should feel more connected to her than anyone he'd known save his own sister. Yet this connection, of course, was *not* the brotherly sort. It was unlike anything he'd known, and he desperately wanted it back.

Wait, maybe he could still get ahold of Ivy. She might be with Marsha Langston. Heck, they worked together. The idea sparked new hope within him. And suddenly he was scrolling back to the unknown number, clicking the call icon, and tapping the screen to put it on speaker. This time it rang.

Once.

Twice.

"Hello, Easton." The expectant tone in the woman's voice made him bristle.

"Marsha," he said, pacing faster now. He wanted to hurry back to the tent and start packing up, but he'd lose reception just a few yards in.

"Thank you for calling," Marsha said.

"Do you know where Ivy is?" he asked. "Is she at work today?"

A quiet pause. "I'm not sure," she finally said. "The poor girl is stuck doing grunt work after the stunt she pulled. She doesn't report directly to me anymore."

Grunt work? Easton gritted his teeth, hating the idea of anyone pushing Ivy around in a job she'd given her life to. *That,* on top of the stupid tabloids?

He forced his mind back to the matter at hand. "What kind of offer do you have? Will it give Ivy her job back? And make the media eat their own words for slandering her name?"

"We might be able to arrange that. But I'd rather not discuss it over the phone. You see, I've never made an offer like this to any prior contestant and I don't plan to in the future. I've got to make sure the deal stays private, which means you'll need to sign an agreement, in person this time."

A fresh dose of irritation pushed through him. "Okay, but did you see the article they published about the runaway bachelor? They basically bash Ivy and put me on some freaking pedestal."

"Which one?"

The two-word question felt like two great swords going clean through him. One from the back—he hadn't expected the first article. And one from the front that he somehow failed to see coming—Easton should have guessed there would be more.

"In order for this to work, I need you here in LA by tonight."

"Perfect." Adrenaline surged through him. Finally an action he could take. One that didn't include wearing a deeper path into the dirt under his boots. "Send me the address and I'll head out now."

"Good. Where are you calling from?"

"Southern Nevada," he answered. "About an hour from the airport."

"You've been camping?" she assumed.

When he didn't answer right away, Marsha continued. "I'll book you the first flight out, arrange for a driver to pick you up from the LA airport, and put you up in the hotel across from the station. If you leave right now, you'll have time to shower, choose from one of the tuxes in your room, and meet me at the network by seven thirty sharp. You'll fly first class; they'll serve you dinner on the way."

This sounded like something with all sorts of strings attached. First class flight? A tux waiting for him at some suite? But who cared if it would lead him to Ivy. To protecting her reputation and name.

"Can you at least tell me if Ivy will be there?"

An extended pause filled the space. Easton pressed the receiver against his ear.

"She will," Marsha finally said. "And I apologize if you've had trouble reaching her. Something's gone amiss with the company phones for a few of our employees. From what I understand, they're not even able to access their contacts anymore. It's terrible. We're trying to fix it."

That explained the automated message. "Let me guess," he said. "Ivy's the only employee whose phone shut off."

"You know, I can't really say," Marsha said in a blasé tone. "But we don't have time for this sort of chat. Get to the airport, get to the studio, and then we can talk."

The line went dead, leaving Easton to his task of packing up and heading out. He broke into a run toward the campground to do just that. At least now he wasn't waiting around and dodging his fate. He'd had enough time to think about what he wanted. And he'd do what it took to get it.

CHAPTER 19

Ivy glanced at the mounding traffic beyond the company's Cadillac limo. Panic built within her as she glanced at the clock beside the crystal glasses and bottles of champagne. It was already 7:15. The preshow started at 7:30, which meant, ideally, they'd be getting seated right now. At least the show itself didn't start until 8:00.

The traffic had gone from slow and steady to stop and go a few miles back. Not a big deal since they'd had plenty of time to get to the station. But over the last half hour, the stops outweighed the go's ten to one. Snails could make laps around them in the time it took to move so much as an inch forward.

"Are Danny and Ronny acting weird?" Jackie asked, brow furrowed as she looked at her phone.

Taya sipped a bit of champagne and grinned. "Weird how?"

"Ronny's being really weird," Joelle affirmed, scrolling along her screen as well. "He said they were going to the game, which doesn't even start for another hour, but suddenly he's saying they're already at the arena and he can't talk."

"Yeah, Paul too," Jackie said. "Mom and Dad said they were going too. Maybe I'll try them."

"What's wrong, Ivy?" Taya asked.

Ivy pulled her gaze off the road. "I'm getting nervous about the traffic. We're supposed to be there in fifteen minutes, but I think it just took us a half an hour to move three feet."'

"Oh, no." Taya ducked her head to look out the windows as well. "I wonder what's going on out there."

"Yeah, me too." But more than that, Ivy wondered what in the world would happen at tonight's show. Would Easton surprise her by showing up after all? It wasn't as if she would know. Not only had her phone service shut down completely, meaning she couldn't receive texts or calls, it had blocked access to her existing contacts.

The only benefit, she decided after going without her phone, was that she could tell herself that Easton might have texted or called her by now. She had no evidence to prove otherwise. But even as she tried to convince herself of that very thing, Ivy knew deep down that he hadn't. And that he probably wouldn't either. The rejection was hard to bear. Sure, she could think back on some of the things he said and come to conclusions that buffered the blow. Like when he'd admitted that he didn't believe in love. But that did little to comfort her. Because Ivy was convinced that he did. And that if he didn't find it with her, he'd surely go on to find it with someone else.

The mature side of her would want that very thing for him. The less developed side of her was another story. Could she handle watching even one episode if Easton actually showed up tonight and went on into the mansion?

No. Definitely not. But would she really be able to resist? And with her job as it was, the whole station would be abuzz with all the things happening on and off screen at the mansion. She could hear it now. *Easton Sparks fell for the vegan chick. He's sworn off meat and vows to only eat tofu until he dies.*

A knot of nausea moved through her stomach. *Come on, traffic. Move!*

It didn't, but the window separating the back cab from the driver did. One slow glide. "I apologize for the wait, ladies. Seems as if there's an accident ahead. It's a few miles up. Once we get past it, we'll be on our way. We're not far from our destination."

"Thank you." Ivy spotted an oversized flatbed truck in front of them. Odd, seeing that it held no cargo at all.

"I hope we make it there in time," Joelle said.

"Me too," Ivy agreed.

"Well, no matter what happens," Taya said, "this has been one incredible day. Let's just sit back, have a little bubbly, and enjoy our time in this amazing limo."

"Good idea," Jackie agreed. She handed Ivy a champagne flute while Taya gave one to Joelle. Joelle's glass, of course, held sparkling cider since she was expecting. "Cheers to sisterhood, unexpected adventures, and...and *Looking For Love!"*

Ivy extended her glass, clinking it gently with each of her sisters, and took a modest sip, recalling the effects of those moonshine peaches. And as she set her gaze out the opposite window, taking in the night skyline of LA with its brilliant city lights, an inquiry came to mind. One she'd been questioning for days. *I wonder where Easton is right now.*

Easton glanced down at his watch as he waited in the greenroom. 7:35. Marsha was late. And for someone who prided herself on timing—she was the producer of several live TV shows, after all—that seemed uncharacteristic.

It didn't help that his mind was treading water in a sea of regret. A sea that was growing deeper and higher with each minute that passed by. He should have given Ivy the benefit of the doubt. She had shown him, during their time together, exactly the type of woman she was.

Ivy was faithful and loyal, a woman who wouldn't betray anyone in such a way. Today, amidst the waves of guilt and remorse crashing about, Easton was finally seeing things clearly now.

The terrible tabloid he'd seen would send any woman into turmoil, there was no doubt. But for someone like Ivy...

A vicious ache tore through him as his eyes clenched closed. For Ivy, it had to be so much worse. She had a warped perception of herself as it was. Of her significance, her worth, and her appeal. They'd talked at length about the ways she'd worked to impress and to prove herself to others. About how her fear of being unimportant or even unlovable had carried into her relationships with men as well. So what else could she conclude when he took off rather than seek her out, except that she wasn't worth the trouble?

He should have been her champion. Instead, he'd been a coward.

That same mean cycle of thoughts fed his desperate urgency to make things right. To tell her—and all of America—that she *was* worth it. He just hadn't dared step up. It was his job to help her see that she was something special, and no matter what it took, no matter what this night held in store, that's what Easton planned to do.

His knee bounced restlessly as he glanced around the room. Empty glasses stood beside a tall pitcher of ice water. He leaned forward and secured a glass. Yet just as he tightened his grip around the icy pitcher, the door burst open.

"You're on," a tall, gawky kid hissed from the door.

Easton set the glass back down. "I'm on…what?"

The kid hurried in and hooked a mic up to Easton's collar. "Say something," he urged.

"What's going on?" he asked.

"Perfect," the kid said. "Lift the back of your tux so I can place the battery pack. It's small, see?" He held up a black box with a clip on the back.

Easton spun around and lifted the tail of the tux. He glanced over his shoulder as he clipped it onto his belt.

"Got it. She's waiting for you out there, so follow me." He hurried toward the door but Easton reached out to grab his arm.

"Wait. Who is?" *Please say Ivy.*

"Marsha," he said over his shoulder. They were moving down a narrow hallway now. One turn left, a quick turn to the right, and suddenly they were at a dead end of sorts. Closed off by a thick, black curtain. The kid spoke something into his mic, eyes set on Easton, then nodded as he gathered whatever response came.

He moved to one side and leaned an ear toward the curtain. "Ten seconds," he mumbled.

The mic. The tux. The curtain. "Am I going on stage?"

The kid brought a finger to his lips. "They're going to turn your mic on any second. And yes, you are. Marsha's hosting the pre-show. She'll be interviewing you live. Good luck."

Interviewing him? On live TV? Panic turned to elation as he realized what that meant. He would get to publicly defend Ivy. In a much bigger way than he'd imagined.

At once, he swung back the curtain, giving Easton his very first glimpse of a live studio audience. Hopefully it would also be his last.

"Go on," whispered the assistant.

Easton stepped onto the stage and glanced to a set of designer lounge chairs surrounding a coffee table. He scanned the area, saw that Ivy wasn't there, and felt his shoulders drop in disappointment.

"Come on over," Marsha coaxed from a high back chair. She stood and motioned to the chair closest to her, each slightly angled toward the audience.

He took a seat as the crowd cheered, then cast a glance over the filled rows. Please say Ivy was there somewhere.

"In less than thirty minutes," Marsha said, eyes set on the camera ahead, "we'll meet the men who are entering the mansion to pursue our five lovely bachelorettes. We'll also meet those bachelorettes and learn—without the guys around—just what they're hoping to find in a man.

"But first, in this special episode, our pre-show to *Looking*

For Love, I'll be playing the part of your host while I interview one particular hopeful who caught my attention. One who," she said, waving a hand in Easton's direction, "caught more than mere attention when he stormed onto the scene. He caught a piece of my very own assistant's heart."

Easton felt like his eyes might pop out of his head at her statement. The audience oohed and ahhed.

"Go ahead, Easton," she urged. "Tell America about how the two of you met."

The contract he'd signed in the green room came to mind. The parts highlighted in yellow stated that he'd need only cooperate by answering a few simple questions. She must have *not* highlighted the part that said those questions would be asked in front of an audience on live TV.

Make it good, Easton. He needed to make it clear that Ivy was capable of winning the heart of any man she chose. He was just lucky enough that it was him.

"Well," he said, recalling their first conversation. "She was coming out to Denver to interview me for the show. I'd, um, lost a bet with my baby sister and, uh..."

"A bet about coming onto the show," Marsha filled in, looking amused instead of angry. *Good thing.*

The audience broke into laughter.

"Yes," he agreed through a laugh of his own. "Knowing she'd land in Denver around the time of a predicted record-breaking blizzard, I warned her that, being close to the holiday as it was, she may end up getting snowed in for Christmas with me. I told her not to fear too much. If that happened, I'd find a way to keep her nice and warm."

An insinuative whistle sounded from the audience, and the crowd broke into laughter once more.

"Who knew," he continued, "that that prediction would come true?"

That one got the crowd really going wild. Easton took the moment to scan over the crowd once more.

Marsha took over. "Let me brag for a moment about what a devoted assistant I have," she said, her gaze turned to the camera. "I'll set the scene. A blizzard is coming. The cab driver tells her no, that he can't drive her up the canyon to Easton's location, which is the nature-focused rehab center he runs for young adults. There's a number on your screen in case you'd like to donate to that organization, by the way," Marsha added slyly. "So Ivy rents an SUV instead." Marsha turned to Easton then. "You were spending the week at the center preparing the huts—"

"Yurts," he said with a nod.

"Yurts, for the winter program. These things have a stable roof, a door, and quite high ceilings from what I hear."

"That's right," he agreed. "Ours also have their own fireplace and venting system."

Marsha grinned. "How *cozy*."

The audience whooped once again.

"I tell you," Marsha said, "if there's one thing I enjoy, it's a good love story. And though Easton was only keeping his word —he'd promised that he would interview for the *Looking For Love* show—this bachelor found love *outside* of the mansion first."

Cat calls and cheers lifted over the crowd.

Easton shifted in his seat.

"We'll hear more about their story after these messages," Marsha assured. "Don't go anywhere."

Easton leaned over his lap as soon as the cameras panned out.

Marsha did the same. "You're doing great," she said.

"Where's Ivy?"

Marsha lifted a finger and tapped at her earpiece. Her brows pulled down in a deep furrow as she seemed to gather a piece of information, and then she lifted her gaze back to him. "Stuck in traffic. There was an accident on the interstate."

"But you planned to have her here?" Easton asked, disappointment pushing its way through him.

"Planned? Yes. I went to great lengths, in fact. An all-day spa treatment, hair, makeup, gowns…It was going to be her own live TV Cinderella story. She deserves that, don't you think?"

Easton couldn't agree more. "Yes, she does."

Marsha frowned. "I thought we'd overcome the biggest feat by getting *you* here in time. But if we can't get Ivy here, the whole thing will be a bust."

Suddenly, the stakes felt higher than ever. Because despite his aversion to being in the public eye, despite his preference for privacy, Easton wanted very badly to give Ivy her own fairytale moment. A happily ever after that, if all went well, would add onto their promising beginning. One they could share with their kids one day. And their kids' kids. They should know that their father, or grandfather as it might be, treated Ivy like a queen.

An idea came to him then. A recollection, really, as he remembered a story Ivy told him once. He motioned Marsha closer as a rush of excitement burst within him.

Marsha leaned in, the smile at her lips saying she sensed he had something that might save the day. She tipped her ear his way, and Easton leaned in further still.

"I've got an idea. But first, tell me this. Is there any way we can get ahold of her father?"

CHAPTER 20

It's no big deal, Ivy. You're just missing the preshow. The traffic will clear up in time for the first episode.

Ivy glanced at the sight before them; that same flatbed truck was still right in front. A green Volkswagen bus remained in the rear. Sure, she wasn't happy about missing the preshow, or the idea of missing the entire live episode, mainly because her sisters were looking so forward to it. But that's not where Ivy's worry lie. Because her real concern, the much greater dilemma, was her relationship with Easton.

Her sisters were content for now; the three of them were admiring one another's gowns, heels, and matching jewelry. She was glad they'd been enjoying the day. And heck, if worse came to worse and they didn't make it to the studio in time for the show, perhaps one of them could try to pull up the live footage on their phone. They could watch it from the limo until they arrived.

She nodded. That might be possible.

Speaking of phones, Ivy mused, spotting something from her periphery. A quick glance at the ladies said she was right—they were each hovered over their phones suddenly. She watched as they exchanged worried glances before shifting their collective gaze to her.

Ivy's heart skipped. "What?"

"Nothing," Taya blurted, shoving her phone on the seat face down.

Joelle stared at her like a deer caught in the crosshairs. "Uh..."

"Joelle's friend just sent her a link," Jackie said, voice filled with dread. "The tabloids got their hands on the story."

Her body was working faster than her brain, it seemed. Because while Ivy struggled to dissect what she'd said, her body was already reacting to the news with a racing pulse.

"What *story?*" she asked.

"The one with you and Easton," her sister explained. "They got it wrong, of course."

"Tabloids are just mean," Taya added. "I wouldn't look at it."

Ivy moved her gaze over the women, catching one sympathetic look after the next. She gulped, humiliation rising so high she could drown in it.

"It's mean?" She wasn't sure how her heart could hammer so wildly. Wasn't it bleeding by now? It felt like it was. In fact, as the sharp and stinging pain swelled with each rhythmic pulse, it felt like it might give out altogether. Taya was definitely right; Ivy shouldn't want to look at it, but she couldn't avoid looking forever.

She extended her hand toward them, bracing herself for

whatever she might see on that screen, and nodded toward Joelle. "Here, can I please see it?"

Suddenly, the distinct sound of a helicopter sounded overhead.

"Must be the station's traffic watch," Jackie guessed.

"Yeah," Taya said.

Distraction was not going to work, Ivy would see to that. But then the sound of the chopper's blades grew louder.

Joelle leaned to get a better look. "That is freaking *loud.* It sounds like it's..." She gasped. "Right next to us!"

"What?" Taya leaned far over next. Ivy and Jackie did the same as the chopper's rhythmic beat grew impossibly louder still, until it echoed throughout the cab.

Ivy covered her ears with her hands. The others did the same.

"What's going on?" Joelle yelled over the noise.

"You've got me," Ivy hollered. That's when she spotted the chopper for herself. Coming right down to land...to land on the center of the massive flatbed in front of them!

"I wonder if someone's hurt," Taya guessed.

"More like in *trouble,*" Jackie said. "That's not life flight; that helicopter belongs to the cops." And there it was, LA County Deputy printed along the side.

The ladies nearly climbed over one another to peek out one corner of the same window, a level of awe filling the space.

It landed completely, right where Ivy had guessed, and then the blades slowed to a stop as the engine shut off.

"This is better than any preshow," Taya said with a laugh.

Joelle leaned in further still. "Tell me about it."

Suddenly the helicopter door dropped open, and a man balancing something on his shoulder stepped out.

"Is that a camera?" Jackie hollered.

"Yes," Ivy realized. "That's exactly what it is. What are they trying to film?"

The suspense only increased as the man aimed the lens on the open door, its bright attachment creating a spotlight of sorts.

"Watch it be Tom Cruise or something," Taya said. "And they're, like, filming a movie."

"That would be awesome," Joelle breathed.

"Totally," Ivy agreed.

Suddenly, a man in what looked like a suit appeared, giving life to Taya's guess.

"He's wearing a tux!" Jackie blurted.

Yes, he was. And he filled it out to perfection. Broad shoulders, a tall build, and…and… Ivy leaned in far enough over to bump the glass with her head. Her eyes had to be deceiving her. But as the spotlight lit up the man's gorgeous face with that chiseled jaw and those deep brooding eyes, she realized that inkling was correct.

"Holy crap," she breathed.

"What?"

"Who is he?"

"Is that an actor?"

She could feel her sisters' eyes on her, but Ivy couldn't take her gaze off the man on the flatbed. The one who was peering right into the limo. Her heart skipped whatever beat it was meant to hit and skittered somewhere high among the clouds.

"No," she answered, shock freezing her very form in place. "It's Easton."

"It's *Easton?*" the three yelled in unison.

"Ivy Ingles," came a voice over the chopper's speaker—the pilot, she guessed. "Please step out of the limo and join Mr. Sparks on the flatbed."

A rush of chills rippled up her arms at the sound of his name—a confirmation that it was, in fact, Easton.

"Oh my gosh!" Taya squealed.

"He is *gorgeous,*" Joelle breathed.

Jackie moved to push open the door. "You better hurry and get out there!"

A great breeze tossed Ivy's hair as she stepped onto the interstate. The surrounding cars had rolled down their windows. An old couple in a convertible two lanes over gave her a wave.

Ivy flattened a hand over her gown; its fabric, caught between silver and white, looked like diamonds in the light. She spun to face the open door where her sisters watched with wide eyes. "How's my hair? And my dress?"

Her heart thundered heavy within her chest.

"*Perfect,*" Taya and Jackie said at the same time.

Joelle nodded. "They're right. You look incredible. This is your night, Cinderella. Go get your prince!"

Ivy bit her lip and spun back around. She knew Easton would be waiting for her there, but the knowledge hadn't prepared her for the sight as he met her gaze. The tux made him look like he'd just stepped off the red carpet. He stood, tall and heroic on the edge of the flatbed, hand extended, eyes fixed right on her.

"Hi," he mouthed as she walked toward him.

"Hi," Ivy mouthed back, careful not to catch her gown on her heels. She reached up, placed her hand in his, and reveled in the wave of warmth and relief that rushed through her at his firm grip.

"Put your foot on the towing hitch there," he instructed with a nod.

She fisted her gown, lifted her foot, and balanced the flat part of her heel on the bar. Yet as Ivy moved to lift her other foot, her gown found its limits.

"I'm pretty sure my dress is going to rip if I move," she said through a nervous laugh.

"Here..." Easton let go of her hand and grabbed hold of her waist. In one quick move, he hoisted her up and onto the flatbed with him, steadying her as she found her footing.

"You look incredible," he breathed.

The light from the camera was aimed right on them, a fact that made her realize what was happening here. This must be part of tonight's live pre-show.

"Thanks," she said, a new rush of nerves coming on. "You, um...look *good* in a tux." That was an understatement. She forced out a slow breath through pursed lips. *Calm, Ivy. Calm.* For all the years she'd spent working for Channel 13, she never imagined being on TV herself.

The thought made her realize what a big deal this was for Easton, someone whose aversion to the cameras was even greater than her own. Yet here he was, holding onto her hands, assuring her with that heroic, save-the-day look in his eyes. Like he had it all under control.

"Ivy," he said as the camera neared. "When I first met you, it was plain to see that you were beautiful, ambitious, and determined. I feared that stubborn determination of yours would make you a real pain in the butt. I was actually terrified to be stuck in the same place with you for even ten minutes."

He chuckled, and so did she.

"But those three days—where we were stuck in that blizzard together—were some of the best days of my life. I saw that you were adaptable, optimistic, funny, bright, and even more beautiful than I'd been able to appreciate before."

Elation washed over her at his words in a warm, glorious wave. A sensation that made her smile broaden even still.

The camera's bright light reflected in Easton's gorgeous brown eyes as he continued, a wry sort of smile forming at his lips. "You're a lightweight when it comes to moonshine, you're an excellent storyteller, and you know *almost* as many geeky fun facts as I do."

"I think I know *more*," she corrected with a laugh.

Easton laughed too and gave her hands a squeeze. "I love that about you." He gulped, searched her face for a blink, his head shaking absently.

"I've been so set on staying single, devoting myself only to the rehab center and my small inner circle, that I never imagined anyone could come in and change that. But you did. For the first time ever, while we were up late talking, making ornaments together, and dancing in the firelight, I pictured doing those things with my wife one day. I pictured *you* being my wife one day, and I liked it." Another wave of appreciation and bliss pushed through her.

Easton wiped a hand over his brow and let out a paced

breath. It was the first time Ivy detected hints of nervousness. She squeezed his hands reassuringly.

"When we said goodbye at the airport, I said that I wasn't sure how we were going to make a relationship work, with you in one state and me in another, but that I wanted to at least try.

"Well, I'm *still* not sure exactly how we're going to do it, but I'm more determined than ever to make it work. Because I want more of you, Ivy. I want to take you on dates, hear more about your past. Get to know your family and have you meet mine. I want to be a part of your life, and hopefully a part of your future too."

He rubbed his thumbs over the back of her hands, tipped his chin down, and looked up at her through his lashes. "I am falling in love with you. Please say you'll forgive me for taking off, and that you'll give me a second chance."

Ivy fought back the squeal of joy that threatened to sound in her throat. Her sisters, on the other hand, let those squeals loose from the limo, a fact that reminded her that they, along with all of America, were watching. The bliss in her body swelled. The sensation so tingly warm and filling, she mused it could lift her feet right off the ground.

The camera man stepped closer.

Ivy licked her lips. "Of course I will, Easton. I'm falling in love with you too."

Crammed cars along the interstate began to honk. Drivers and passengers began to cheer. The lights on the helicopter flashed, and a chain reaction picked up in both directions as far as the eye could see.

Ivy giggled. "This is amazing," she breathed.

"Well, what are you waiting for?" the pilot asked through the speaker. "Go ahead and kiss the girl."

Easton grinned as his face flushed red. He pulled her into him then, his smile fading as his expression turned serious. "I don't mind if I do." He pressed his full, wonderful lips to hers then, thrilling her with a sensation Ivy had feared she might never feel again.

More cheers came as she wrapped her arms around him and reveled in his kiss.

She pulled back slightly, looked into his eyes once more, and smiled.

It was then that Marsha stepped out of the helicopter, a wide grin on her face, and waved the cameraman out of her way. And were those tears she was wiping from her eyes? The cameraman turned the lens on Marsha, leaving Ivy and Easton with some off-camera time to themselves. Well, and the hundreds of people surrounding them on the interstate.

"Is Marsha letting you off the hook?" Ivy asked.

He nodded. "She's even raising money for the center right now, during the live broadcast."

Wow, the woman really was a romantic, wasn't she? "Is she the one responsible for the tux? If so, I'll have to thank her."

Easton nodded and grinned. "The tux was her doing. But, well, *I* was going for the whole squad car thing, but your dad said the chopper would be a better way to go."

"My *dad?"* Her eyes widened.

Easton took that time to explain that her parents, and her brothers too, were waiting at the studio for them, which meant they were watching it all unfold on a big screen among hundreds of fans. She couldn't help but take satisfaction in the fact.

Soon, the traffic would clear and they'd head to the studio for the rest of the premier. Also soon, they'd discuss what the short-term future would look like for them, dating as they planned to do. But for now, Ivy would enjoy the splendid heaven of Easton Spark's embrace, and bask in the redemption, the joy, and the hope he'd given her.

Easton had gone to great lengths to make this happen. He'd come out of hiding, given up his privacy, and made a major public display.

And in the moment of bliss, among the night sky, their audience in cars, and the warm California wind, Ivy basked in the knowledge that, in Easton's mind, Ivy was worth a gesture so grand. And something told her that this was only the start. *Their* start, to a happily ever after.

EPILOGUE

"Wanna hear something cool?" Easton asked while he lay next to Ivy by the fireplace. It was her turn to visit him, and late spring in Denver could still get rather chilly, especially for her.

"Let me guess," Ivy said. "You're going to tell me that it takes twelve pounds of milk to produce just one gallon of ice cream?"

Easton chuckled, glancing at their empty ice cream containers on the mantle. "I hadn't heard that one before. Guess that means I'm going to have to pee soon."

Ivy chuckled and gave him a nudge. "What were you going to say?"

"Just that, now that the baby's born, Chantelle says she wants to open the second nature rehab center."

"That's awesome."

Yes, it was. Thanks to Marsha's more than generous donation—and the fundraiser she'd kept running during the entire first episode—they'd raised enough money to make it happen.

He and Ivy's social media page, something Ivy created after the show, continued to bring in donations as well.

"Guess where we're going to put the new center."

Ivy bit her lip and looked off in the distance, eyes narrowing in concentration. But then suddenly she gasped, sat up straight, and turned a very serious look on him. "Easton!" Her eyes were the size of saucers.

He grinned. "What?" His tone came out playful. He was enjoying this, after all.

"Is it…" She covered her mouth, as if she didn't dare even speak it, then blinked twice, then pulled her hand down. "Are you going to build it in LA?" Her body turned jittery as she waited for his reply, as if she'd just stepped into a frigid storm.

"Tell me," she pleaded, grabbing his arm and rocking him back and forth.

A chuckle escaped Easton's lips. "Yes, Ivy. Of course we're building it there. We'll all be moving there too because…" He shifted himself up and onto one knee, then reached for the small box he'd tucked behind the wood stack. He cracked it open to reveal the ring and set his gaze back on Ivy. "Because I'd like you to marry me."

Ivy squealed at the sight of the ring. Before he could brace himself, she flung her arms around him and squeezed him tight.

Easton wrapped his arms around her in return. Her exuberant reaction was just as he'd hoped it might be. "Is that a yes?" he asked, his mouth very close to her ear.

"You know it is." Ivy giggled, pulled back, and framed his face with her hands. Her blue eyes were wide and bright. "I'd *love* to marry you, Easton." She moved in to kiss him then, a slow and lingering kiss. One that promised all the things he hoped to do with her once she was officially his.

Heat roared low in his belly as she caught his bottom lip between hers and pulled back, ever so gently.

"I, uh..." he stammered once his lips were free, "...should have asked you a long time ago."

Ivy giggled, then came in for another sensual, drawn out kiss.

"I'm not kidding," he said, making her laugh again.

He flattened one hand along her back and moved it slowly up to her neck. The soft and silky feel of her skin beneath his palm made his mouth water. Slowly then, Easton moved in to press kisses over the delicate hollow of her throat, allowing his heated breath to tease her between each kiss.

Ah, yes, there's that whimper I like to hear.

She gripped at his arms, and his pulse spiked.

Barely suppressing the urgency within him, Easton started a teasing trail of kisses up the side of her neck. He sampled the soft lobe of her ear, desperate to kiss her lips once more, when suddenly something tumbled from his hand. The ring box.

That reminded him—she'd said yes. And it was time to get that ring on her finger. "I almost forgot," he whispered against her skin. "Let's try that ring on for size."

He forced himself to release the warm splendor in his arms and reached out to secure the box. His proposal wasn't entirely out of the blue. The two had started talking about marriage once they confessed their love for each other. Her sisters had been looking at rings with her for quite some time and her selection never wavered.

"That's the most beautiful ring I've ever seen…in person," she added with a grin.

"Then your sisters didn't lead me astray," he said. "Chantelle is going to freak out when she sees you wearing it." They were headed over there for dinner soon. "We should wait and see who notices first. Her, Tim, or the baby."

Ivy grinned. "Baby Easton will probably point it out first. Two-month-olds are good at spotting details like that," she joked.

"Man, I can't wait to hold that little guy," Easton admitted.

"Me neither."

In the light and heat of the flames, Easton pulled the dainty ring from the blue velvet box and balanced it between his finger and thumb. He glanced up at the woman he loved, the very one who'd changed his life in every possible way, and cleared his throat as his emotions gripped hold of him hard. Enough that moisture welled up in his eyes.

Less than one year ago, Easton couldn't have pictured himself vowing his life to someone. But here he was, thrilled to be doing that very thing. He'd noticed a change in his work at the center too. As the young adults spoke of their uncertainty about marriage and love, Easton could speak from experience about his shift in perspective. About opening up to it when the right person came. And they *would* come, he felt safe to assure them. When the timing was right, they would come.

He slid the ring onto Ivy's finger, his heart filled with more love than he knew what to do with, and looked into her eyes. "Do you know how the ring finger became the ring finger?" He'd been waiting to share this one.

Ivy bit her lip, reached out to wipe a tear from his upper

cheek, and shook her head. "No." A small laugh coated her reply. "How?"

He traced a line up the back of her finger. "Before medical science knew how things worked, people thought there was a vein running directly from this fourth finger on your left hand, straight into the heart. Because of that hand-heart connection, they named the vein *vena amoris*. That's Latin for *vein of love*."

Ivy wiped a tear from her own cheek now. "That will forever be my favorite fun fact of all."

Easton had to agree. He moved in to kiss her lips once more, thrilling from the truth in his head—he and Ivy would share a life together. They'd no doubt encounter their share of blizzards, but at least now, as the years came, went, and brought what they may, he and Ivy would weather the storms *together*.

SAMPLE CHAPTER

Thank you for reading Snowed In For Christmas. Keep reading the clean romance with this sample chapter of *28 Days With a Billionaire* from the best-selling Benton Brothers Series also by Kimberly Krey.

28 Days With a Billionaire

Chapter 1 (sample)

Camila counted the empty dinner plates before her for the millionth time.

Thirteen. There would now be thirteen guests for Mr. Shimwah's dinner party instead of eleven. Sparks of panic flared hot beneath her cool façade.

Twelve would have been fine. Twelve would have put her exactly *one* over the expected amount of guests and—as America's finest culinary institute had drilled into her—planning for an extra guest was imperative.

But two?

She glanced through the spotless floor-to-ceiling windows and onto the scenic LA patio where Ricco Shimwah, one of the world's fastest rising fashion designers, entertained his guests. The late evening sun glistened off the ocean in shades of orange and gold, a perfect contrast to the turquoise water and white, crashing waves.

She'd give just about anything to be on the other side of that glass tonight, kicking back with a drink while the ocean breeze swept over her skin.

Normally Camila enjoyed her role as a private chef—preferred it, even. It's what she'd always dreamt of—serving her own culinary creations to LA's elite. But the pressure of the evening was taking its toll.

Two extra dishes. She groaned. *Please say Gypsy is scoring those quail eggs.*

Her phone buzzed on demand, the very sound fanning the anxious flares coursing through her. Camila shot a look at Mr. Shimwah, who was tipping his head back in laughter from the conversation. Quickly, she dashed into the walk-in pantry, pried the phone from her apron pocket, and brought it to her lips without even checking the screen; she already knew who it was.

"Did you find them?" Her heart beat wildly out of rhythm as she waited for her reply.

"Tell me again why you can't just use a freaking chicken egg like the rest of the universe?"

Now Camila was the one tipping her head back, one step closer to madness. "They cover too much of the plate," she explained in a hush. "Quail eggs are like, a third of the size, which allows the croquettes to shine since *they*'re the main event. The egg's just a compliment."

"So this is all about how it looks?" Gypsy asked. "Not how it tastes?"

"It's about both." Though, in truth, the taste didn't vary much between the two. "And if you know me and you know what I do, you also know how important presentation is."

"Yeah, yeah," Gypsy grumbled. "You eat with your eyes first."

Camilla paced before the fridge—an industrial appliance reserved for staff— hoping to ease the coil-like tightening around her throat, when suddenly a male voice caught her off guard.

"Oh, my apologies. I thought…"

She spun in place to see who'd entered the pantry of all places and set eyes on a handsome guest dressed in what had to be a tailored-just-for-him suit. Her gaze drifted up to his face. Strong, chiseled jaw, heavenly blue eyes, and a brooding, almost sad quality that hung somewhere behind his expression.

Camila gulped, a swell of tingly heat pooling around her heart.

Please say this tall spot of gorgeousness isn't Mr. Shimwah's new boyfriend. Sure, he was probably in his mid-twenties, like Camila, but the fifty-something year-old designer often dated guys half his age.

"I thought this was the restroom." He cleared his throat and pointed a thumb over one broad shoulder. "Shimwah said it'd be the first on my right beyond the kitchen."

The man's arresting gaze held hers as the moment stretched

on, giving life to the sadness she'd seen there. He was rattled about something, it was clear.

"Hellooooo..." Gypsy sang into the phone.

"Just a second," she mumbled under her breath. Camila gave the guest a soft smile. "I um... yeah, it's probably the *second* one down."

The handsome man gave her a curt nod, spun right in place, and strode out. It was then Camila realized he'd called his host *Shimwah* instead of Ricco–definitely not the boyfriend. But who was he? And just what was bothering him?

"Are you there?" Gypsy whistled into the phone.

"Yeah." Camila's shoulders went limp. She would probably never have answers to those questions, and right now she had a job to do. "I'm here."

"Good. Cuz I've got your quail eggs."

It took at least two seconds to set her mind back on the issue at hand. "You got them?" she squealed.

Gypsy gave her a hard *tsk* through the line. "Of course I got them. I just...wanted to know why you needed them so bad, that's all."

Relief rushed through her limbs in a blink. "Thank heavens. And you did *not* just want to know why I needed them. You wanted to make me suffer. Admit it."

"I might be twisted," Gypsy said, "but I'm not *that* sick. I took time away from my beach meditation for you."

"Bless you for that, sweet Gypsy. I owe you big." Camila tugged open the fridge where the salad plates chilled. It was almost time to serve up the first course: bright beet ginger kraut on a gorgeous bed of mixed greens. The herb-infused vinaigrette was waiting at room temperature in the prep area, allowing for the perfect drizzle consistency. All was ready to go.

"Okay, I think I'm nearing his estate," Gypsy said. "Wow, it's *huge!*"

Camilla nodded and closed the fridge. "You haven't seen the half of it. Park on the left hand side of the gate entrance. I'll head out and meet you." It was easier than pulling Shimwah away from his guests to grant her entry.

She snuck out an exit in the back of the house, one leading to the staff's quarters, and hurried down a winding, stone-covered staircase.

"Man, this place is incredible," her friend hissed. "I'm bummed I didn't come with you on this one."

"Yeah, but if you had, you probably wouldn't have been able to save my bacon like this."

"True."

Camilla spotted her friend waiting beside the gated entrance. Platinum, shoulder length hair with a blue streak down the side, that beach wave giving life to a name that suited her so well. Carefree. Fun. Go with the flow.

Camilla's more traditional style of long brown hair with blonde highlights spoke to her personality as well. More structured, disciplined, or, as Gypsy often accused, boring.

"Royal quail eggs for your royal guests," Gypsy said as she lifted the sack toward her. "May they feast like kings."

Her sarcasm made Camilla grin. "Thank you, fair peasant. May you find fortune in the next life, as I see it escaped you in this."

Gypsy giggled. "Hey, now. We're *both* peasant girls, and don't you forget it."

Camilla steadied the paper sack with both hands, careful to slide it between the iron bars without incident, and brought her face close. Gypsy pressed her cheek in the open space, and Camilla planted a kiss there. "Now go, before the king's men find you."

Camila's list of last minute to-dos ran through her mind as she carefully weaved through the plush landscape and back to the path. She held the carton of eggs, tucked into a shallow paper bag, like a platter of champagne glasses before her, gliding up the windy outdoor stairwell with paced and precise steps. It seemed like the smart way to carry them until she reached the top of the stairs and—*slam*—crashed into something moving faster than she was.

Or some*one.*

The impact knocked her off balance, forcing Camila's weight to tip until she hovered backward over the stairs she'd just climbed.

A horrified gasp tore from her throat.

Her chest clenched tight.

And for a split second, she was forced to choose: save herself or preserve the very precious item in her hands. Her brain was too foggy to recall what that item was, she only knew she needed to protect it at all cost. A task that became impossible as a strong hand gripped hold of her arm, forcing whatever it was to tumble out of her hands and onto the red-glazed stone paving the stairs.

"Careful," the man growled. "Didn't you see the handrail?"

Camila shot a look at the grip he had on her arm, realizing it was the only thing that kept her from falling, but the man was quick to release it and take a step back. *Oh, no. It was pantry guy, wasn't it?*

She moved her gaze up his familiar looking build. A pair of black suit pants, a crisp, white-collared shirt over broad shoulders, and a black tie. Maybe it wasn't pantry guy. *He'd* been wearing a suit coat.

"You nearly fell down that entire flight of stairs," he snapped, causing her gaze to shoot to his face next. Ice blue eyes, squared jaw, and an angry furrow at his brow. *Ugh.* It *was* him.

She forced out the only word that leapt to her tongue as she remembered what lay in a heap on the ground between them.

"Eggs. The eggs. I *really* need them." She hunched down to retrieve the goods, groaning when she realized the bag had tipped upside down during the fall. Was it possible at least one egg survived?

"Is *that* what's on my sleeve?"

Camila had heard what he'd said, but she was too busy prying open the crumpled carton to reply. Raw egg dripped from each tiny shell, answering her question with gruesome finality.

"I knew I shouldn't have removed my suit coat," he grumbled.

Camila forced her gaze off the sad remains in time to see a slimy looking yolk, bright yellow against the white, dripping over a silver cufflink where tiny diamonds spelled out the initials JB.

"You should really try and watch where you're going. I'll be stuck wearing that stuffy suit coat to cover this up for the remainder of the night."

Anger flared in her chest. "And *I'll* be stuck serving one of tonight's meals without a quail egg," she snapped back.

The man's face scrunched up. "*Quail?*" He looked like a finicky kid who'd been served a plate of broccoli minus the cheese. "Hold the disgusting quail egg on my dish, and everyone will be happy. Okay?"

A part of Camila was relieved, there was no doubt about it. But another part of her was stuck on his bossy tone. "Oh, so I'm taking orders from you now? I don't think Mr. Shimwah would appreciate that. Unless *you're* the guy he's dating..."

The man offered his hand to her, chuckling under his breath in what sounded like genuine amusement.

After a blink of hesitation she took hold of his solid wrist.

He hoisted her back to her feet with one effortless tug, but the momentum forced her to bump right into his chest.

"Nice try," he said as she took a step back. "I'm sure you know exactly who I am, which means you also know that I'm *not* dating Mr. Shimwah." He lifted those broad shoulders back into place. "I am, however, here with his top model, Adel Bordeaux."

Was *he* the second extra guest?

He gave her a curt nod. "Good luck with your meal. I look forward to it, now that it won't have a quail's egg on it." With that, he proceeded down the winding staircase, hints of his spicy aftershave lingering in the breeze.

Camila stared down at the mess in his wake. She'd assumed, after their run-in at the pantry, that he was a decent guy. Wrong. He was pompous. And rude. And most of all, *wrong* about her knowing who he was.

"For your information," she hollered over her shoulder. "I have no idea who you are."

He was out of sight now, but a low chuckled bounced off the glazed staircase. "Mmm, hmm."

Camila rolled her eyes, mumbling something she knew he wouldn't hear. "Sorry, buddy. You're not as *famous* as you'd like to think."

This completes the sample chapter of 28 Days With a Billionaire. To keep reading, click link: 28 days with a Billionaire.

FREE BOOK

Subscribe to my newsletter and receive my novella, Ranch Hand for Auction, FREE as a thank you gift!

ALSO BY KIMBERLY KREY

Unlikely Cowgirl Series

Her Gun-shy Cowboy

Her Kismet Cowboy

Her Dream Cowboy

Cobble Creek Small Town Romance

The Unlikely Bride

The Hopeful Bride

The Determined Bride

The Sweet Montana Bride Series

Reese's Cowboy Kiss

Jade's Cowboy Crush

Cassie's Cowboy Crave

Second Chances Series

Rough Edges

Mending Hearts

Fresh Starts

Beach Romance

Catching Waves: A Sweet Beach Romance (The Royal Palm Resort Book 2)

28 days with a Billionaire

Benton Brothers Romance

28 days with a Billionaire

Her Best Friend Fake Fiancé

Stepping In For The Billionaire Groom

The Billionaire's Second Chance

The Billionaire's (Not So) Fake Engagement

Young Adult Novellas

Getting Kole for Christmas

Getting Micah under the Mistletoe

Chemistry of a Kiss

Novella

Ranch Hand for Auction

Navy SEALs Romance

The Honorable Warrior

The Fearless Warrior

Christmas Romance

Her TV Bachelor Fake Fiancé

Her Best Friend Fake Fiancé

The Billionaire's (Not So) Fake Engagement

Snowed In For Christmas

Getting Kole for Christmas

Getting Micah under the Mistletoe

The Comfy Christmas Collection: Four Holiday Romance Reads; First Loves & Second Chances

Collections

Falling for Her Bodyguard: Four Full-length Romance Novels

Cobble Creek Romance Collection: Three small-town Romances

The Sweet Montana Bride Series: Three Witness Protection Cowboy Romances

Second Chance Romance Series: Three Sweet Romances Featuring Second Chances

Falling for the Cowboy Collection: Unlikely Cowgirl Series - 3 Western Romance Novels

It All Starts Here: Sweet Romance Collection

Someone To Love

Wrapped In Romance Collection

Worth The Fight

Under One Roof

Benton Brothers Billionaire Romance Collection

Also See

The Cowboy's Catch (in Big Sky Anthology)

ABOUT THE AUTHOR

Writing Romance That's Clean Without Losing the Steam!

Award-winning author Kimberly Krey specializes in writing 'Romance That's Clean without Losing the Steam'. She's a fervent lover of God, family, and cheese platters, as well as the ultimate hater of laundry. Subscribe to her newsletter and follow her on any of the sites below for updates on new releases and or giveaways.

facebook.com/kimberlykreyauthor
twitter.com/KimberlyKrey
instagram.com/romance_is_write
bookbub.com/profile/kimberly-krey

CREDIT/ACKNOWLEDGMENTS

Fun fact about taste buds: https://www.nectarsleep.com/posts/fun-facts-about-the-human-body/

Fun fact about tongue muscles: https://www.mentalfloss.com/article/570937/facts-about-the-human-body

Fun fact about Eye muscles: https://www.guinnessworldrecords.com/world-records/420629-fastest-human-muscle

Fun facts about Jingle Bells: https://www.pastbook.com/txt/12-fun-christmas-facts/

Fun fact about fire: https://capepoint.co.za/fun-facts-about-fires/

Fun facts about airplanes: https://www.kiwi.com/stories/15-fun-facts-airplanes-flying-surprise-you/

Fun fact about ring finger: https://www.google.com/search?client=firefox-b-1-d&q=why+ring+finger%3F